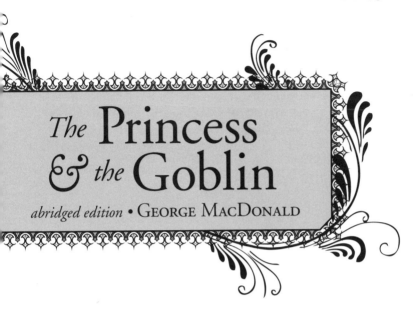

*The* Princess
& *the* Goblin

*abridged edition* • GEORGE MACDONALD

JOURNEYFORTH
Greenville, South Carolina

**Library of Congress Cataloging-in-Publication Data**

MacDonald, George, 1824-1905.
    The princess and the goblin / George MacDonald. — Abridged ed.
      p. cm.
    Sequel: The princess and Curdie.
    Summary: A little princess is protected by her friend Curdie and her
newly-discovered great-great-grandmother from the goblin miners who
live in caves beneath the royal castle.
    ISBN-13: 978-1-59166-799-5 (perfect bound pbk. : alk. paper)
    [1. Fairy tales.]  I. Title.
    PZ8.M1754Pr 2007
    [Fic]—dc22

                                                  2007026550

Design by Craig Oesterling
Page layout by Kelley Moore

© 2007 BJU Press
Greenville, SC 29614
JourneyForth is a division of BJU Press

ISBN 978-1-59166-799-5

15   14   13   12   11   10   9   8   7   6   5   4   3   2   1

# Publisher's Note on The Value of Good Fantasy

Fantasy is defined as any story of the impossible, a tale including events that contradict the laws of the natural world.

One of the functions of good fantasy is to remove life's problems from their normal setting and thereby throw their causes and solutions into relief, making the lessons easier to recognize and remember. When the reader leaves the story and goes back about his ordinary life, he has with him some clearer understanding of principles by which to make choices and judgments.

The first important fantasies specifically for children appeared in the nineteenth century. Hans Christian Andersen, in addition to retelling traditional tales, wrote original fanciful stories heavily influenced by folk tradition. His popularity inspired others, including George MacDonald, and, by the last half of the nineteenth century, many writers were experimenting with this form.

The writings of George MacDonald, in turn, inspired C. S. Lewis. Lewis wrote in his preface to *George MacDonald: An Anthology*, "I have never concealed the fact that I regarded him as my master; indeed I fancy I have never written a book in which I did not quote from him."[1]

---

[1] C. S. Lewis, *George MacDonald: An Anthology*. (New York: Macmillan, 1947), 20.

For Lewis, MacDonald was more a Christian teacher than a literary model. He said that MacDonald was the greatest writer of a kind of fantasy that is at once both allegory and myth and that what MacDonald's work "actually did to me was to convert . . . my imagination."[2]

Writers like MacDonald and Lewis use their converted imaginations to reinforce Christian truths. In their works, the reader enters a world far different from his own, where he encounters treachery and deception and fear—as well as great compassion, Truth, and courage. He learns there a Christian worldview; he learns that authority must reside in powers higher than himself, and that when power is wrested from authority, it always results in disaster.

Some are suspect of fantasy because it seems unreal and because it sometimes contains elements other writers have used badly. All genres and all symbols and all styles have been used by the ungodly for ungodly purposes since the beginning. In the garden of Eden, Satan turned God's own words to his wicked intent and used them to undermine Eve. Fantasy, the genre, is not evil; it is only the uses some put it to that are evil.

Ironically, fantasy is one of the best means of helping students learn literary skills that will make them recognize good writing of any kind. Set apart from the ordinary world, elements in fantasy stand out in bold relief—a wax mask is much more clearly a symbol of deceit than, say, a shifty look. Learning to recognize and interpret such symbols will help

[2]Ibid., 21.

young readers understand they must be aware that whatever they read is sending a message to be evaluated.

Fantasy well handled can often make a point that will be more memorable than in a realistic setting because students respond to that which delights. Entertainment is a good teaching tool, so long as there is more than entertainment to be had when all is said and done. Superior imaginative writing recognizes the playfulness that all children possess, but it also recognizes the duty of literature to present truth.

The presence of the badly done fantasy more than ever necessitates the availability of good fantasy. Young people who are presented with good reading of many kinds and who are taught to recognize the elements that make a book good will not be satisfied with lesser books or vulnerable to it for lack of experience. They will be wise and thoughtful readers all their lives.

# CONTENTS

# WHY THE PRINCESS HAS A STORY ABOUT HER

There was once a little princess whose father was king over a great country. His land was full of mountains and valleys, and upon one of the mountains his palace was built. The palace was very grand and beautiful. Princess Irene was born there, but because her mother was not very strong, she was sent soon after her birth to be brought up by country people in a large house which was half castle and half farmhouse. It stood on the side of another mountain about halfway between its base and its peak.

The princess was a sweet little creature about eight years old. Her face was fair and pretty with eyes like two sparkling bits of night sky. Those eyes must have known where they came from, so often were they turned upward. The ceiling of her nursery was blue with stars in it, as like the sky as they could make it, though it is doubtful that she ever saw the *real* sky with the stars in it. And here is the reason.

These mountains were full of hollow places within—huge caverns and winding ways, some with water running through them, and some shining with all the colors of the rainbow in the light. There would not have been much known about them, had there not been mines there. Great deep pits with long galleries and passages running off from them had been dug to get to the ore of which the mountains were full. In the course of digging, the miners came upon many of these natural caverns. A few of them had far-off openings out on the side of a mountain or into a ravine.

In these subterranean caverns lived a strange race of beings, called by some gnomes, by some kobolds, and by some goblins, or cobs for short. There was a legend in the land that at one time they lived above ground and were very like other people. But for one reason or another, the king had laid severe taxes upon them, or had required observances they did not like, or had begun to treat them with more severity in some way or other, and imposed stricter laws. The consequence was that they had all disappeared from the face of the country.

According to the legend, instead of going to some other country, they had all taken refuge in the subterranean caverns. They never came out except at night, and then they seldom showed themselves in any numbers and never to many people at once. It was only in the least frequented and most difficult parts of the mountains that they were said to gather even at night in the open air.

Those who had caught sight of any of them said that they had greatly changed in the course of generations. It was no wonder, seeing that they lived away from the sun in cold and wet and dark places. They were now not simply ugly, but they were either absolutely hideous, or ludicrously grotesque both in face and form. There was no invention of the wildest imagination that could outdo their awful appearance, though it may be that sometimes the goblins themselves were mistaken for their animal companions.

The goblins were not so far removed from humans as such a description would imply. But as they grew misshapen in body, they had grown in knowledge and cleverness. They were now able to do things no mortal could possibly do. But as they grew in cunning, they also grew in mischief. Their great delight was to annoy, in every way they could think of, the people who lived in the open air above them. They had enough affection left to preserve them from being absolutely cruel for cruelty's sake. But still they so heartily cherished the ancestral grudge against the descendants of the king, that they sought every opportunity of tormenting them in ways that were as odd as their inventors. Although dwarfed and misshapen, they had strength equal to their cunning. In the process of time they got their own king and a government too, whose chief business, beyond their own simple affairs, was to devise trouble for their neighbors.

And so it should be fairly evident why the little princess had never seen the sky at night. There was too much fear of the goblins to let her out of the house then, even in company of ever so many attendants.

And it will be seen that they had good reason.

## 2

# THE PRINCESS LOSES HERSELF

his is how Princess Irene's story begins.

One very wet day the mountain was covered with mist which was constantly gathering itself together into raindrops, pouring down on the roofs of the great old house to fall in a fringe of water from the eaves all round about it.

The princess could not of course go out. She got very tired, so tired that even her toys no longer amused her. So she sat in the nursery with the sky ceiling over her head, at a great table covered with her toys. Her back bowed into the back of the chair, her head hung down, and her hands rested in her lap. She was very miserable, not even knowing what she would like to do, except to go out and get thoroughly wet. Yet if she got particularly wet, she would likely catch a cold and have to go to bed and eat gruel.

Then her nurse left the room, and Irene tumbled off her chair and ran out as well, not through the same door the nurse went out, but another one which opened at the foot of a curious old stair of worm-eaten oak. It looked as if no one had ever set foot upon it. And that seemed sufficient reason on such a rainy day for trying to find out what was at the top of it.

Up and up she ran—such a long way it seemed to her!—until she came to the top of the third flight. There she found the end of a long passage, and into this she ran. The hall was full of doors on each side, so many that she did not care to open any, but ran on to the end. There she turned into another passage, also full of doors. When she had turned twice more and still saw doors and only doors about her, she began to get frightened. It was so silent save for the rain which made a great trampling noise on the roof. Irene turned back and started to run at full speed, her footsteps echoing through the sounds of the rain. She ran back to the stairs and the safety of her nursery. Or so she thought. But she had lost herself long ago. It doesn't follow that she should be lost, but indeed she was.

She ran for some distance, turned several times, and then began to be afraid. Very soon she *knew* that she had lost her way. Rooms everywhere, and stairs nowhere. Her heart beat as fast as her feet ran, and a lump began to grow in her throat. At last her hope failed her. Nothing but passages and doors everywhere, and she threw herself on the floor and burst into a wailing cry.

She did not cry long, however, for she was as brave as could be expected of a princess of her age. And so after a good cry, she got up and brushed the dust from her frock. What old dust it was! She wiped her eyes with her hands, for she didn't have her handkerchief in her pocket.

Then, like a true princess, she wisely resolved to work her way back. She would walk slowly through all of the passages and search in every direction for the stair. This she did, but without success. She went over the same ground again and again without knowing it, for the passages and doors were all alike. At last, in a corner through a half-open door, she did see a stair. But sadly, it went the wrong way. Instead of going down, it went up. Frightened as she was, however, she could not help wishing to see where the stair would lead. It was very narrow, and so steep that she climbed it like a four-legged creature on her hands and feet.

# 3

# THE PRINCESS AND—
# WE SHALL SEE WHO

When she came to the top, she found herself in a little square place with three doors. Two were opposite each other, and one was in front of her at the top of the stair. She stood for a moment without an idea in her head of what to do next.

But as she stood, she began to hear a curious humming sound. Could it be the rain? No. It was much more gentle and even more monotonous than the sound of the rain which now she scarcely heard. The low sweet humming sound went on, sometimes stopping for a little while and then beginning again. It was like the hum of a bee that had found a rich well of honey in some flower. Where did it come from? She laid her ear first to one of the doors to listen there—then to another. When she laid her ear against the third door, there could be no doubt where it came from. It was something in that room. She was rather afraid, but her curiosity was stronger than her fear, so she opened the door very gently and peeped in. A very old lady sat spinning.

The princess could tell that the lady was an *old* lady. She was beautiful, and her skin was smooth and white. Her hair was combed back from her forehead and face, and it hung loose far down and all over her back, white almost as snow. And although her face was smooth, her eyes looked so wise that you could not have helped seeing she must be old. The princess, though she could not have told you why, did think her very old indeed—*quite fifty*, she said to herself. But the lady was even older than that.

While the princess stared bewildered with her head just inside the door, the old lady lifted hers and spoke in a sweet, but old and rather shaky voice. It mingled very pleasantly with the continued hum of her wheel.

"Come in, my dear; come in. I am glad to see you."

That the princess was a real princess was quite plain, for she didn't hang onto the handle of the door and stare without moving. She did as she was told, stepped inside the door at once, and shut it gently behind her.

"Come to me, my dear," said the old lady.

And again the princess did as she was told. She approached the old lady rather slowly, but she did not stop until she stood by her side. Irene looked up into the lady's face with her own blue eyes with the two melted stars in them.

"Why, what have you been doing with your eyes, child?" asked the old lady.

"Crying," answered the princess.

"Why, child?"

"Because I couldn't find my way down again."

"But you could find your way up."

"Not at first. Not for a long time."

"But your face is streaked like the back of a zebra. Hadn't you a handkerchief to wipe your eyes with?"

"No."

"Then why didn't you come to me to wipe them for you?"

"Please, I didn't know you were here. I will next time."

"There's a good child," said the old lady.

Then she stopped her wheel and rose. She left the room and returned with a little silver basin and a soft white towel, with which she washed and wiped the bright little face. And the princess thought her hands were so smooth and nice.

When the old lady carried away the basin and towel, the little princess wondered to see how straight and tall she was. Although she was so old, she didn't stoop a bit. She was dressed in black velvet with thick white lace about it. And her hair shone like silver. There was hardly any more furniture in the room than there might have been in that of the poorest old woman who made her living by her spinning. There was no carpet on the floor; no table anywhere; nothing but the spinning wheel and the chair beside it. When she came back, she sat down and without a word began her spinning once more. Irene, who had never seen a spinning wheel, stood by her side and looked on.

When the old lady had got her thread fairly going again, she said to the princess, but without looking at her, "Do you know my name, child?"

"No, I don't," answered the princess.

"My name is Irene."

"But that's *my* name!" cried the princess.

"I know that. I let you have mine. I haven't got your name. You've got mine."

"How can that be?" asked the princess, bewildered. "I've always had my name."

"Your papa, the king, asked me if I had any objection to your having it; and, of course, I hadn't. I let you have it with pleasure."

"It was very kind of you to give me your name—and such a pretty one," said the princess.

"Oh, not so very kind," said the old lady. "A name is one of those things one can give away and keep at the same time. I have a good many such things. Wouldn't you like to know who I am, child?"

"Yes—very much."

"I'm your great-great-grandmother," said the lady.

"What's that?" asked the princess.

"I'm your father's mother's father's mother."

"Oh, dear! I can't understand that," said the princess.

"I didn't expect you would. But that's no reason why I shouldn't say it. I will explain it all to you when you are older," the lady went on. "But you will be able to understand this much now: I came here to take care of you."

"Is it long since you came? Was it yesterday? Or was it today, because it was so wet that I couldn't get out?"

"I've been here ever since you came yourself."

"What a long time," said the princess. "I don't remember it at all."

"No. I suppose not."

"But I never saw you before."

"No. But you shall see me again."

"Do you live in this room always?"

"I don't sleep in it. I sleep on the opposite side of the landing. I sit here most of the day."

"I wouldn't like that. If you are my great-great-grandmother, then you must be a queen too."

"Yes, I am."

"Where is your crown then?"

"In my bedroom."

"I would like to see it."

"You shall some day. Not today."

"I wonder why Nurse never told me."

"Nurse doesn't know. She never saw me."

"But somebody knows that you are in the house?"

"No; nobody."

"How do you get your dinner then?"

"I keep poultry—of a sort."

"Where?"

"I will show you."

"Who makes the chicken broth for you?"

"I never kill any of my chickens."

"Then I can't understand."

"What did you have for breakfast this morning?" asked the lady.

"I had bread and milk, and an egg. I dare say you eat their eggs."

"Yes, that's it. I eat their eggs."

"Is that what makes your hair so white?"

"No, my dear. It's old age. I am very old."

"I thought so. Are you fifty?"

"More than that."

"Are you a hundred?"

"More than that. I am too old for you to guess. Come and see my chickens."

Again she stopped her spinning. She rose, took the princess by the hand, led her out of the room, and opened the door opposite the stair. The princess expected to see a lot of hens and chickens, but instead of that, she saw the blue sky first, and then the roofs of the house with a multitude of the loveliest pigeons, mostly white, but of all colors. They were walking about, making bows to each other, and talking a language she could not understand. She clapped her hands with delight, and up rose such a flapping of wings that she in her turn was startled.

"You've frightened my poultry," said the old lady, smiling.

"And they've frightened me," said the princess, smiling too. "But what very nice poultry! Are the eggs nice?"

"Yes, very nice."

"What a small egg spoon you must have! Wouldn't it be better to keep hens, and get bigger eggs?"

"How would I feed them though?"

"I see," said the princess. "The pigeons feed themselves. They've got wings."

"Just so. If they couldn't fly, I couldn't eat their eggs."

"But how do you get at the eggs? Where are their nests?"

The lady took hold of a little loop of string in the wall at the side of the door and, lifting a shutter, showed a great many pigeonholes with nests, some with young ones and some with eggs in them. The birds came in at the other side, and she took out the eggs on this side. She closed it again quickly, lest the young ones should be frightened.

"Oh, what a nice way!" cried the princess. "Will you give me an egg to eat? I'm rather hungry."

"I will some day, but for now you must go back, or Nurse will be miserable about you. I dare say she's looking for you everywhere."

"Except here," answered the princess. "Oh, how surprised she will be when I tell her about my great-great-grandmother!"

"Yes, that she will!" said the old lady with a curious smile. "Mind you, tell her all about it exactly."

"That I will. Please, will you take me back to her?"

"I can't go all the way, but I will take you to the top of the stair, and then you must run down quite fast into your own room."

The little princess put her hand in the old lady's, who, looking this way and that, brought Irene to the top of the first stair, and then to the bottom of the second. She did not leave the princess until they were halfway down the third.

When the old lady heard the nurse's cry of pleasure at finding Irene, she turned and walked up the stairs again, very fast indeed for such a very great-great-grandmother. And she sat down to her spinning with a strange smile on her sweet old face.

# 4

# What the Nurse
# Thought of It

"Where you have been, Princess?" asked Nurse, taking the girl in her arms. "It's very unkind of you to hide away so long. I began to be afraid." Here she stopped.

"What were you afraid of, Nurse?" asked the princess.

"Never mind," she answered. "Perhaps I will tell you another day. Now tell me where you have been."

"I've been a long way up the stairs to see my very great, huge, old grandmother," said the princess.

"What do you mean by that?" asked the nurse, who thought she was making fun.

"I mean that I've been a long way up and up to see my great-great-grandmother. Ah, Nurse, you don't know what a beautiful mother of grandmothers I've got upstairs. She is such an old lady with such lovely white hair—as white as my silver cup. Now, when I think of it, I think her hair must be silver."

"What nonsense you are talking, Princess!" said Nurse.

"I'm not talking nonsense," returned Irene, rather offended. "I will tell you all about her. She's much taller than you, and much prettier."

"Oh, I dare say!" remarked Nurse.

"And she lives upon pigeons' eggs."

"Most likely," said Nurse.

"And she sits in an empty room, spinning all day long."

"Without a doubt," said the nurse.

"And she keeps her crown in her bedroom."

"Of course—quite the proper place to keep her crown. She wears it in bed, I'll guess."

"She didn't say that. And I don't think she does. That wouldn't be comfortable, would it? I don't think my papa wears his crown for a nightcap, does he?"

"I never asked him."

"And she's been there ever since I came here. Ever so many years."

"Anybody could have told you that," said Nurse, who did not believe a word that Irene was saying.

"Why didn't you tell me then?"

"There was no need to. You could make it all up for yourself."

"You don't believe me!" exclaimed the princess, astonished and angry, as she well might be.

"Did you expect me to *believe* you?" asked Nurse coldly. "I know princesses are in the habit of telling make-believes, but you are the first I ever heard of who expected to have them believed," she added, seeing that the child was strangely in earnest.

The princess burst into tears.

"Well, I must say," remarked Nurse, now thoroughly vexed with Irene for crying, "that it is not at all becoming to tell stories and expect to be believed just because you are a princess."

"But it is quite true, I tell you."

"You've dreamt it then, child."

"No, I didn't dream it. I went upstairs, and I got lost, and if I hadn't found the beautiful lady, I would never have found my way back."

"Oh, I dare say!"

"Well, you just come with me then, and see if I'm not telling the truth."

"Oh, no. I have other work to do. It's your dinner time, and I won't have any more such nonsense."

The princess wiped her eyes, and her face grew so hot that they were soon quite dry. She sat down to her dinner, but ate next to nothing. Not to be believed does not at all agree with princesses. So all afternoon she did not speak a word—except for when Nurse spoke to her, for a real princess is never rude.

Of course Nurse did not suspect the least truth in Irene's story, but she loved her dearly and was vexed with herself for being cross with her. She thought her crossness was the cause of the princess's unhappiness and had no idea that Irene was really and deeply hurt at not being believed. But it became more and more plain during the evening in Irene's every motion and look that although she tried to amuse herself with her toys, her heart was too troubled to enjoy them.

The nurse's discomfort grew and grew. When bedtime came, she dressed and laid the princess down in bed. But the child, instead of holding up her face up to be kissed, turned away and lay still. Then Nurse's heart gave way altogether, and *she* began to cry. At the sound of her first sob, the princess turned again and held her face to be kissed as usual. But the nurse had her handkerchief to her eyes and did not see the movement.

"Nurse," said the princess, "why won't you believe me?"

"Because I can't believe you," said Nurse, getting angry again.

"Ah, well then. If you *can't* help it," said Irene, "I will not be vexed with you any more. I will give you a kiss and go to sleep."

"You little angel!" cried Nurse.

"You will let me take you to see my dear old great-great-grandmother, won't you?" asked the princess.

"I will go with you anywhere you like, my dear," Nurse answered. And in two minutes the weary little princess was fast asleep.

5

# THE PRINCESS LETS
# WELL ALONE

When she woke the next morning, the first thing
she heard was the rain still falling. This day
was quite like the last, but the first thing she
thought of was not the rain, but the lady in the tower. The
first question that occupied her thoughts was whether she
should ask Nurse to go with her to find her grandmother as
soon as she had eaten her breakfast. She came to the conclusion that perhaps the old lady would not be pleased if she took
anyone to see her without first asking permission; especially
as it was pretty evident, seeing she lived on pigeons' eggs, that
she did not want the household to know she was there. So the
princess resolved to take the first opportunity of running up
alone and asking whether she might bring her nurse.

The princess and her nurse were the best of friends again,
and the princess ate an enormous breakfast.

"I wonder, Lootie"—that was her pet name for Nurse—"what
pigeons' eggs taste like?" she said, as she was eating her egg.

"We'll get you a pigeon's egg, and you shall decide for yourself," said the nurse.

"Oh, no, no!" returned Irene, suddenly thinking that they might disturb the old lady getting an egg, and that she would have one less to eat as a result.

"What a strange creature you are," said Nurse—"first to want an egg and then to refuse it."

But she did not say it crossly, and the princess never minded remarks that were not unfriendly.

"Well, Lootie, there are reasons," she returned and said no more. She did not want to bring up the subject of their former strife, lest Nurse should offer to go with her before she had her grandmother's permission. Of course the princess could refuse to take her, but then Nurse would believe her less than ever.

Now the nurse could not be in the room every moment, and before yesterday the princess had not given her the smallest reason for anxiety, and so it had not yet come into her head to watch Irene more closely. So at the very first opportunity, Irene was off and up the stairs again.

This day's adventure, however, did not turn out like yesterday's, although it began quite like it. The princess ran through passage after passage and could not find the stair to the tower. When she turned to go back, she failed equally in her search for the stair. She was lost once more.

Something made it even worse to bear this time, so it was no wonder that she cried again. Then it occurred to her that it was after having cried before that she had found her grandmother's stair, so she got up at once, wiped her eyes, and started upon a fresh quest.

This time, although she did not find what she hoped, she found what was next best. She did not come to a stair that went up, but she came upon one that went down. It was not the stair she had come up, yet it was a good deal better than none. So down she went singing merrily, when to her surprise, she found herself in the kitchen. Although she was not allowed to go there alone, her nurse had often taken her there, and she was a great favorite with the servants. There was a general rush at her the moment she appeared, for everyone wanted her. The report of where she was soon reached Nurse's ears, and she came at once to fetch her. She never suspected how the princess had gotten there, and the princess kept her own counsel.

Irene's failure to find the old lady not only disappointed her, but made her very thoughtful. Sometimes she came almost to Nurse's opinion that she had dreamed it all, but that fancy never lasted very long. She wondered whether she would ever see the old lady again, and thought it very sad not to have been able to find her. She resolved to say nothing more to her nurse on the subject, seeing she had so little to prove her words.

## 6

# THE LITTLE MINER

The next day the great cloud still hung over the mountain, and rain poured like water from a full sponge. The princess was very fond of being out of doors, and she nearly cried when she saw that the weather was no better. But the mist was not a dark dingy gray; there was light in it, and as the hours went on it grew brighter and brighter. Late in the afternoon the sun broke out gloriously.

"See, Lootie! Look how bright it is! Do get my hat, and let us go out for a walk."

Lootie was very glad to please the princess. She got her hat and cloak, and they set out together for a walk up the mountain. The clouds were rolling away in broken pieces like great, woolly sheep. Between them the sky shone with a deep pure blue. The trees on the roadside were hung all over with drops, which sparkled in the sun like jewels. The only things that were no brighter for the rain were the brooks that ran down the mountain, and they had changed from crystal clear to a muddy brown. But what they lost in color, they gained in sound, or at least in noise, for a brook when it is swollen is not so musical as before. But Irene was delighted with the great brown streams tumbling down everywhere. Nurse shared in her delight, for she too had been confined to the house for three days.

Finally Nurse observed that the sun was getting low, and although she said it was time to be going back, the princess begged her to go on just a little farther. The princess reminded Nurse that it was much easier to go downhill so that when they did turn back, they would be home in a moment. So on and on they went to look at a group of ferns or to pick up a shining rock by the wayside or to watch the flight of some bird. Suddenly the shadow of a great mountain peak loomed up in front of them. When Nurse saw it, she caught hold of the princess's hand, turned, and began to run down the hill.

"What's all the haste, Nurse?" asked Irene, running alongside her.

"We must not be out a moment longer."

"But we can't help being out a good many moments longer."

It was true, and the nurse almost cried for they were much too far from home. It was against express orders to be out with the princess one moment after the sun was down, and they were nearly a mile up the mountain! If His Majesty, Irene's papa, were to hear of it, Nurse would certainly be dismissed. It was no wonder she ran. But Irene was not in the least bit frightened, not knowing anything to be frightened about. She kept on chattering as well as she could, but it was not easy.

"Lootie, why do you run so fast? It shakes my teeth when I talk."

"Then don't talk," said Lootie.

But the princess went on talking, and Lootie paid no more heed to anything she said, only ran on.

"Look, Lootie! Do you see that funny man peeping over the rock?"

Lootie ran faster. They had to pass the rock, and when they came nearer, the princess saw it was only a lump of the rock itself that she had taken for a man.

"Look, Lootie. There's a curious creature at the foot of that old tree. Look at it, Lootie! It's making faces at us, I think."

Lootie ran faster still—so fast that Irene's little legs could not keep up with her, and she fell with a crash. It was a hard downhill road, and she had been running very fast, so it was no wonder she began to cry. Nurse was nearly beside herself, but all she could do was to run on the very moment she got the princess back on her feet again.

"Who's that laughing at me?" said the princess, trying to keep in her tears and running too fast for her grazed knees.

"Nobody, child," said Nurse, almost angrily.

But that instant there came a burst of coarse laughter from somewhere near, and a hoarse indistinct voice that seemed to say, *Lies! lies! lies!*

"Nurse! I can't run any more. Do let us walk a bit."

"Here, I will carry you," said Nurse.

She took her up, but found her much too heavy to run with and had to set her down again. Then she looked wildly about her, gave a great cry, and said, "We've taken a wrong turn somewhere, and I don't know where we are. We are lost!"

The terror she was in quite bewildered Irene. It was true enough that they had lost the way and had run into a little valley where there was no house to be seen.

But since the servants all had strict orders never to mention the goblins to princess, she did not know the reason for Nurse's terror. It was very disconcerting to see such fright, but before the princess had time to grow thoroughly alarmed, she heard the sound of whistling. Presently she saw a boy coming up the road from the valley to meet them. He was the whistler. But before they met, his whistling changed to singing.

And this is what he sang:

> "Ring! Dod! Bang!
> Go the hammers' clang!
> Hit and turn and bore!
> Whizz and puff and roar!
> Thus we rive the rocks,
> Force the goblin locks.
> See the shining ore!
>
> "One, two, three—
> Bright as gold can be!
> Four, five, six—
> Shovels, mattocks, picks!
> Seven, eight, nine—

Light your lamp at mine.
Ten, eleven, twelve—
Loosely hold the helve.

"We're the merry miner boys,
Make the goblins hold their noise."

"I wish *you* would hold your noise," said Nurse rudely, for the very word *goblin* at such a time and in such a place made her tremble. It would most certainly bring the goblins upon them, she thought, to defy them in that way. But whether the boy heard her or not, he did not stop his singing.

"Thirteen, fourteen, fifteen—
This is worth the siftin';
Sixteen, seventeen, eighteen—
There's the match, and lay't in.
Nineteen, twenty—
Goblins in a plenty."

"Do be quiet," cried the nurse.
But the boy, who was now close at hand, still went on.

"Hush! Scush! Scurry!
There you go in a hurry!
Gobble! Gobble! Goblin!
There you go a wobblin';
Hobble, hobble, hobblin—
Cobble! Cobble! Cobblin'!
Hob-bob-goblin!—Huuuuuh!"

"There!" said the boy, as he stood still opposite them. "There! That'll do for them. They can't bear singing, and they can't stand that song. They can't sing themselves, for they have no more voice than a crow; and they don't like other people to sing."

The boy was dressed like a miner with a curious cap on his head. He was a very nice-looking boy with eyes as dark as the mines in which he worked and as sparkling as the crystals in their rocks. He was about twelve years old. His face was quite pale, which came of his being so little in the open air and sunlight. But he looked merry indeed—perhaps at the thought of having routed the goblins—and his bearing as he stood before them had nothing clownish or rude about it.

"I saw them," he went on, "as I came up, and I'm very glad I did. I knew they were after somebody, but I couldn't see who it was. They won't touch you so long as I'm with you."

"Why, who are you?" asked Nurse, offended at the freedom with which he spoke to them.

"I'm Peter's son."

"Who's Peter?"

"Peter the miner."

"I don't know him."

"I'm his son though."

"And why should the goblins mind you?"

"Because I don't mind them. I'm used to them."

"What difference does that make?"

"If you're not afraid of them, then they're afraid of you instead. And I'm not afraid of them. That's all. And that's all that's needed—up here, that is. It's a different thing down there. They don't always heed that song down there. And if anyone sings it, they grin at him awfully. If he gets frightened and misses a word or says a wrong one, they—oh, don't they give it to him then!"

"What do they do to him?" asked Irene, with a trembling voice.

"Don't go frightening the princess," said Nurse.

"The princess," repeated the little miner, taking off his curious cap. "I beg your pardon, but you oughtn't to be out so late. Everybody knows that's against the law."

"Yes, indeed it is!" said Nurse. "And I shall have to suffer for it."

"Indeed, for it must be your fault," said the boy. "But it really is the princess who will suffer for it. I hope they didn't hear you call her the princess. If they did, they're sure to recognize her again. They're awfully sharp."

"Lootie!" cried the princess. "Take me home."

"Don't go on like that," said Nurse to the boy, almost fiercely. "How could I help it? I lost my way."

"Well, you shouldn't have been out so late. You wouldn't have lost your way if you hadn't been frightened," said the boy. "Come along. I'll soon set you right again. Shall I carry your little Highness?"

"Impertinence," murmured Nurse, but she did not say it aloud, for she thought if she made him angry he might take his revenge by telling someone at the house, and then it would be sure to come to the king's ears.

"No, thank you," said Irene. "I can walk very well, though I can't run so fast as Nurse. If you will give me one hand, Lootie will give me another, and then I shall get on famously."

They soon had her between them holding a hand of each.

"Now let's run," said Nurse.

"No, no!" said the little miner. "That's the worst thing you can do. If you hadn't run before, you would not have lost your way. And if you run now, they will follow you in a moment."

"I don't want to run," said Irene.

"You don't think of me," said Nurse.

"Yes, I do, Lootie. The boy says they won't touch us if we don't run."

"Yes, but if they know at the house that I've kept you out so late, I shall be turned away."

"Turned away? Lootie, who would turn you away?"

"Your papa, child."

"But I'll tell him it was all my fault. And you know it was, Lootie."

"He won't believe that. I'm sure he won't."

"Then I'll go down on my knees and beg him not to take away my own dear Lootie."

The nurse was comforted at hearing this and said no more. They went on, walking pretty fast, but taking care not to run a step.

"I want to talk to you," said Irene to the little miner, "but I don't know your name."

"My name's Curdie, little princess."

"What a funny name! Curdie. What more?"

"Curdie Peterson. What's your name, please?"

"Irene."

"What more?"

"I don't know what more. What more is my name, Lootie?"

"Princesses haven't got more than one name. They don't need it."

"Well, then, Curdie, you must call me just Irene and no more."

"No, indeed," said Nurse indignantly. "He shall do no such thing."

"What shall he call me, then, Lootie?"

"Your Royal Highness."

"My Royal Highness? What's that? No, no, Lootie. I don't like to be called names. You told me once yourself it's only rude children that call names, and I'm sure Curdie wouldn't be rude. Curdie, my name's Irene."

"Well, Irene," said Curdie, with a glance at the nurse which showed he enjoyed teasing her, "it is very kind of you to let me call you anything. I like your name very much."

He expected the nurse to interfere again; but he soon saw that she was too frightened to speak. She was staring at something. It was a few yards before them in the middle of the path, where it narrowed between rocks so that only one could pass at a time.

"It is very kind of you to go out of your way to take us home," said Irene.

"I'm not going out of my way yet," said Curdie. "It's on the other side of those rocks that the path turns off to my father's."

"You won't leave us till we're safe home, I'm sure," gasped Nurse.

"Of course not," said Curdie.

"You dear, kind Curdie! I shall give you a kiss when we get home," said the princess.

The nurse gave her a great pull by the hand she held. But at that very instant the something in the middle of the path began to move. One after another it shot out four long things, like two arms and two legs, but it was now too dark to tell what they were. The nurse began to tremble from head to foot. Irene clasped Curdie's hand yet tighter, and Curdie began to sing again.

"One, two—
Hit and hew!
Three, four—
Blast and bore!

"Five, six—
There's a fix!
Seven, eight—
Hold it straight!

"Nine, ten—
Hit again!
Hurry! Scurry!
Bother! Smother!

"There's a toad
In the road!
Smash it! Squash it!
Fry it! Dry it!

"You're another!
Up and off!
There's enough!—
Huuuuuh!"

As he uttered the last words, Curdie let go of the princess and rushed at the thing in the road as if he would trample it under his feet. It gave a great spring and ran straight up one of the rocks like a huge spider. Curdie turned back laughing and took Irene's hand again. She grasped his hand very tightly, but said nothing until they had passed the rocks. A few yards more and she found herself on a part of the road she knew and was able to speak again.

"Do you know, Curdie, I don't quite like your song. It sounds rather rude to me," she said.

"Well, perhaps it is," answered Curdie. "I never thought of that; it's a way we have. We do it because they don't like it."

"Who don't like it?"

"The cobs. That's what we call the goblins."

"Don't!" said Nurse.

"Why not?" said Curdie.

"I beg you don't. Please."

"If you ask me that way, of course, I won't; though I don't know why. Look! There are the lights of your great house down below. You'll be at home in five minutes now."

Nothing more happened, and they reached home in safety. Nobody had missed them or even known they had gone out. So they arrived at the door to their part of the house without anyone seeing them. The nurse rushed a hurried good night to Curdie, caught Irene by the hand, and dragged her safely within.

"Lootie! I promised a kiss," cried Irene.

"A princess mustn't give kisses to miner boys. It's not at all proper," said Lootie.

"He's a brave boy, and he has been very kind to us, Lootie, and I promised."

"Then you shouldn't have promised."

Lootie did not know which the king might count the worst—to let the princess be out after sunset or to let her kiss a miner boy.

"Never mind, Princess Irene," he said. "You needn't kiss me tonight, but you needn't break your word either. I will come another time."

"Oh, thank you, Curdie," said the princess.

"Good night, Irene. Good night, Lootie," said Curdie, and he turned and was out of sight in a moment.

"I should like to see him come again," muttered Nurse as she carried the princess to the nursery.

"You will," said Irene. "You may be sure Curdie will keep his word."

"I should like to see him!" repeated Nurse and said no more, not wanting to open a new cause of strife with the princess by saying more plainly what she really did mean. She was glad enough that she had succeeded both in getting home unseen and in keeping the princess from kissing the miner's boy. She resolved to watch her far better in the future, for her carelessness had already doubled the danger she was in.

Formerly the goblins were her only fear; now she had to protect her charge from Curdie as well.

## 7

# THE MINES

Curdie went home whistling and resolved to say nothing about the princess for fear of getting her nurse into trouble. Although he had enjoyed teasing her, he was careful not to do her any harm. He saw no more of the goblins and was soon fast asleep in his bed.

When he woke in the middle of the night, he heard curious noises outside. He sat up and listened, then got up, and quietly went out the door. When he peeped around the corner, he saw under his own window a group of stumpy creatures. He recognized the goblins at once by their shape. He had hardly begun his *One, two, three!* when they scurried away out of sight. He laughed, returned to bed again, and was fast asleep in a moment.

Reflecting on the matter in the morning, he came to the conclusion that since nothing of the kind had ever happened before, they must be annoyed with him for interfering to protect the princess. By the time he was dressed, however, he was thinking of something quite different, for he was not worried about the goblins in the least. As soon as he and his father had eaten breakfast, they set off together for the mine.

They entered the hill through a natural opening under a huge rock where a little stream rushed out, and they followed its course where it took a turn and sloped steeply into the heart of the hill. With many angles and windings and branchings-off, it led them deep into the hill until they arrived at the place where they were presently digging out the mountain's precious ore.

With flint and steel and tinderbox they lighted their lamps, then fixed them on their heads, and were soon hard at work with their pickaxes and shovels and hammers. Father and son were at work near each other, but not in the same gang—the passages out of which the ore was dug, they called *gangs*—for when the lode, or vein of ore, was small, one miner would have to dig away alone in a passage only big enough to work. Sometimes they dug in uncomfortable cramped positions. If they stopped for a moment, they could hear the sounds of their companions burrowing away in all directions inside the great mountain. Some were boring holes in the rock in order to blow it up with gunpowder, others were shoveling the broken ore into baskets to be carried to the mouth of the mine, and still others were chipping away with their pickaxes. Sometimes a miner in a very lonely part would hear only a *tap-tapping*, no louder than that of a woodpecker, for the sound would come from a great distance off through the solid mountain rock.

The work was hard, for it is very warm underground; but it was not particularly unpleasant. Some of the miners, when they wanted to earn a little more money for a particular purpose, would stay behind the rest and work all night. They could not tell night from day down there, except for feeling tired and sleepy; for no sunlight came into those gloomy regions. Some who had worked all during the night would declare the next morning that every time they halted for a moment to take breath, they heard a *tap-tapping* all about them even though they were certain there were none of their companions at work. It was as if the mountain were more full of miners than during the day.

But some miners would *never* stay overnight, for all knew those were the sounds of the goblins who worked only at night. For the goblins' *day* was the miners' night. In fact a great number of the miners were afraid of the goblins. There were strange stories well-known of the treatment some miners had received from the goblins during their work at night. The more courageous miners, however, Peter Peterson and Curdie among them, had stayed in the mine all night time and again. Although they had several times encountered a few stray goblins, they had never yet failed in driving the cobs away with verse, for the goblins hated poems of every kind. The miners who were most afraid of goblins were those who could neither make verses themselves nor remember ones that other people made for them. Those who were never afraid were those who could recite verses for themselves. Although there were certain old rhymes which were very effectual, it was well-known that a new rhyme of the right sort was even more distasteful to the cobs, putting them to flight.

Curdie had decided that if his father would permit him to remain there alone this night he would save his extra wages that he might buy a very warm, red petticoat for his mother, who had begun to complain of the cold of the mountain air sooner than usual this autumn. He also had just a faint hope of finding out what the goblins were about under his window the night before.

When Curdie told this to his father, there were no objections. His father had great confidence in his boy's courage and resources.

"I'm sorry I can't stay with you," said Peter; "but I want to go and pay the parson a visit this evening, and besides I've had a bit of a headache all day."

Curdie was the only one who remained in the mine that night. About six o'clock all the rest went away bidding him good night and telling him to take care of himself, for he was a great favorite with them all.

"I'll keep a sharp lookout, I promise you," said Curdie.

"Don't forget your rhymes," said one.

"No, no," answered Curdie.

"It's no matter if he does," said another, "for he'll only have to make up a new one."

"Yes; but he mightn't be able to make it fast enough," said yet another; "and while it was cooking in his head, they might take a mean advantage and set upon him."

"I'll do my best," said Curdie. "I'm not afraid."

"We all know that," they returned.

And they left Curdie alone in the mine.

# 8

# The Goblins

For some time Curdie worked away, throwing all the ore he disengaged on one side behind him to carry out in the morning. He heard a good deal of goblin tapping, but it all sounded far away in the hill, and he paid it little heed. Towards midnight he began to feel rather hungry, so he dropped his pickaxe and got out a lump of bread which in the morning he had laid in a damp hole in the rock.

He sat down on a heap of ore and ate his supper. Then he leaned back for five minutes' rest before beginning his work again and laid his head against the rock. He had not kept the position for a full minute before he heard something which made him sharpen his ears. It sounded like a voice inside the rock. After a while he heard it again. It was a goblin voice—no doubt about that—and this time he could make out the words.

"Hadn't we better be moving?" it said.

A rougher and deeper voice replied, "There's no hurry. That wretched little mole won't break through tonight, if he work ever so hard. He's not by any means at the thinnest place."

"But you still think the lode does come through into our house?" said the first voice.

"Yes, but a good bit farther on than he has got to yet. If he had struck a stroke more to the side just here," said the goblin, tapping the very stone against which Curdie's head lay, "he would have been through. But he's a couple of yards past it now, and if he follow that lode, it will be a week before it leads him in. You see it back there? A long way. Still, perhaps in case of accident it would be as well to be getting out of here now. Helfer, you'll take the great chest. That's your business, you know."

"Yes, Father," said a third voice. "But you must help me to get it on my back. It's awfully heavy, you know."

"It isn't just a bag of smoke, I admit. But you're as strong as a mountain, Helfer."

"You say so, Father. I think myself I'm all right. But I could carry ten times as much, if it wasn't for my feet."

"That is your weak point, I confess, my boy."

"Ain't it yours too, Father?"

"To be honest, feet are a goblin weakness. Why they come so soft, I declare I haven't an idea."

"Specially when our heads are so hard."

"Yes, my boy. The goblin's glory is his head. To think how the fellows up above there have to put on helmets and things when they go fighting. Ha, ha!"

"But why don't we wear shoes like them, Father? I should like to when I've got a chest like that on my head."

"It's not the fashion. The king never wears shoes."

"The queen does."

"Yes; but that's for distinction. The king's first wife wore shoes because she came from upstairs. And when she died, the next queen did not wish to be inferior to her, so she chose to wear shoes too. It was all pride. She forbids them to the rest of the women."

"I'm sure I wouldn't wear them. No, that I wouldn't!" said the first voice, which was evidently that of the mother of the family. "I can't understand why either of them should."

"Simply because the first queen was from upstairs," said the other. "That was the only silly thing I ever knew His Majesty guilty of. Why would he marry an outlandish woman like that—one of our natural enemies too?"

"I suppose he fell in love with her."

"Pooh! He's just as happy now with one of his own people."

"Did she die very soon? They didn't tease her to death, did they?"

"Oh, dear, no! She died when the young prince was born."

"We never do that. It must have been because she wore shoes."

"I don't know that."

"Why *do* they wear shoes up there?"

"Ah, now that's a sensible question, and I will answer it. But in order to do so, I must first tell you a secret. I once saw the queen's feet."

"*Without* her shoes?"

"Yes—without her shoes. And what do you think? She has toes!"

"Toes. What's that?"

"You may well ask. The ends of her feet were split up into five or six thin pieces."

"Oh, horrid! How could the king have fallen in love with her?"

"You forget that she wore shoes. And that is just why she wore them. That is why all the men, and women too, upstairs wear shoes. They can't bear the sight of their own feet without them."

"Ah, now I understand."

"If ever you wish for shoes again, Helfer, I'll hit your feet—I will."

"No, no, mother; pray don't."

"Then don't you."

"Well, I never knew so much before," remarked a fourth voice.

"Your knowledge is not universal quite yet," said the father. "You were only fifty last month. Mind you, see to the bed and bedding. As soon as we've finished our supper, we'll be up and going. Ha! ha! ha!"

"What are you laughing at, husband?"

"I'm laughing to think what a mess the miners will find themselves in."

"What do you mean?"

"Nothing."

"Yes, you do mean something. You always do mean something."

"It's more than you do, then, wife."

"That may be; but it's not more than I find out, you know."

"Ha! ha! You're a sharp one. What a mother you've got, Helfer!"

"Yes, Father."

"Well, I suppose I must tell you. They're all at the palace consulting about it tonight; and as soon as we've got away from this thin place, I'm going there myself to hear what night they fix upon. I should like to see that young ruffian there on the other side, struggling in the agonies of—"

He dropped his voice so low that Curdie could hear only a growl. The growl went on in the low bass for a good while as inarticulate as if the goblin's tongue had been a sausage. It was not until his wife spoke again that it rose to its former pitch.

"But what shall we do when you are at the palace?" she asked.

"I will see you safe into the new house I've been digging for you for the last two months. Podge, I commit the table and chairs to your care. The table has seven legs—each chair three. I shall entrust them all to your hands."

After this arose a confused conversation about the various household goods and their transport, and Curdie heard nothing more that seemed of any importance.

He now knew at least one of the reasons for the constant sound of the goblin hammers and pickaxes at night. They were making new houses for themselves to which they might retreat when the miners threatened to break into their dwellings.

But he had learned two things of far greater importance. The first was that some grievous calamity was almost ready to fall upon the heads of the miners. The second was the knowledge of the one weak point of a goblin's body—their feet were exceedingly tender. He had heard it said that they had no toes, but since he had never had opportunity of inspecting them closely, for it was in the dusk that they always appeared, he could not satisfy himself whether that fact was correct. Indeed, he had not been able even to satisfy himself as to whether they had no fingers, although that also was commonly said to be the fact.

But what was of most importance was the fact concerning the softness of the goblin feet—a fact that might be useful to all miners. In the meantime, however, he had to discover, if possible, the special evil plan the goblins had now in their heads.

Although he knew all the gangs and natural galleries in the mined part of the mountain, he had not the least idea where the palace of the king of the gnomes was. Had he known the whereabouts of the palace, he would have set out at once on the enterprise of discovering what the goblins' plan was. He judged, and rightly, that it must lie in a farther part of the mountain, and that there was as yet no connection between it and the mine. There must be one gang nearly completed, however; for it could be but a thin partition which now separated them.

If only he could get through in time to follow the goblins as they retreated. A few blows would doubtless be sufficient—perhaps just where his ear now lay. But if he attempted to strike there with his pickaxe, he would only hasten the departure of the goblin family, put them on their guard, and perhaps lose their involuntary guidance. He therefore began to feel the wall with his hands, and he soon found that some of the stones were loose enough to be drawn out with little noise.

Laying hold of a large one with both his hands, he drew it gently out, and set it down softly.

"What was that noise?" said the goblin father.

Curdie blew out his light lest it should shine through.

"It must be that one miner that stayed behind the rest," said the mother.

"No; he's been gone a good while. I haven't heard a blow for an hour. Besides, it wasn't like that."

"Then I suppose it must have been a stone carried down the brook inside."

"Perhaps."

Curdie kept quite still. After a little while, hearing nothing but the sounds of their preparations for departure, mingled with an occasional word of direction, and anxious to know whether the removal of the stone had made an opening into the goblins' house, he put in his hand to feel. It went in a good way and then came in contact with something soft. He had but a moment to feel it as it was very quickly withdrawn. It was the foot of one of the toeless goblins! The owner of it gave a cry of fright.

"What's the matter, Helfer?" asked his mother.

"A beast came out of the wall and licked my foot."

"Nonsense! There are no wild beasts in our country," said his father.

"But it was, Father. I felt it."

"Nonsense, I say. Will you malign your native realms and reduce them to a level with the country upstairs? Up there it is swarming with wild beasts of every description."

"But I did feel it, Father."

"I tell you to hold your tongue. You are no patriot."

Curdie suppressed his laughter and lay still as a mouse—but no stiller, for every moment he kept nibbling away with his fingers at the edges of the hole. He was slowly making it bigger, for here the rock had been very much shattered with a blasting.

To judge from the mass of confused talk which now and then came through the hole, there seemed to be a good many in the family. And when all were speaking together, it was just as if they had bottlebrushes in their throats. It was not easy to make out much that was said. At length he heard once more what the father goblin was saying.

"Now, then," he said, "get your bundles on your backs. Here, Helfer, I'll help you up with your chest."

"I wish it was *my* chest, Father."

"Your turn will come in good time! Make haste. I must go to the meeting at the palace tonight. When that's over, we can come back and clear out the last of our things before the enemies return in the morning. Now light your torches, and come along. What a privilege it is to provide our own light, instead of being dependent on a thing hung up in the air—a most disagreeable contrivance—intended no doubt to blind us when we venture out under its baleful influence! Quite glaring and vulgar, I call it, though no doubt useful to poor creatures who haven't the wit to make light for themselves."

Curdie could hardly keep himself from calling through to know whether they made even their own fire to light their torches by. But a moment's reflection showed him that they would have said they did, inasmuch as they struck two stones together, and the fire came.

## 9

# THE HALL OF THE GOBLIN PALACE

A sound of many soft feet followed, but soon ceased. Then Curdie flew at the hole like a tiger, and tore and pulled. The sides gave way, and it was soon large enough for him to crawl through. He did not betray himself by rekindling his lamp, but the torches of the retreating company lined up in a straight long avenue from the door of their cave, threw back light enough to afford him a glance around the deserted home of the goblins.

To his surprise, he could discover nothing to distinguish it from an ordinary natural cave into which the rest of the miners had come in their excavations. The goblins had talked of coming back for the rest of their household gear, but he saw nothing to make him suspect a family had taken shelter there for even a single night. The floor was rough and stony; the walls were full of projecting corners; the roof in one place stood twenty feet high, and in another endangered his forehead. On one side a stream no thicker than a needle trickled down the face of the rock, but still was sufficient to spread a wide dampness over the wall.

The goblin troop in front of him was toiling under heavy burdens. He could distinguish Helfer now and then in the flickering light with his heavy chest on his bending shoulders. The second brother was almost buried in what looked like a great feather bed.

*Where do they get the feathers?* thought Curdie.

In a moment the troop disappeared at a turn of the way, and it was now both safe and necessary for Curdie to follow them lest they should round the next turn before he saw them again and lost them altogether. He darted after them like a greyhound. When he reached the corner and looked cautiously around, he saw them again at some distance down another long passage.

None of the galleries he saw that night bore signs of the work of man—or of goblin either. Stalactites, far older than the mines, hung from their roofs. And their floors were rough with boulders and large round stones, showing that water must have once run there.

He waited again at a corner until they had disappeared around the next, and so followed them a long way through one passage after another. The passages grew more and more lofty and were draped from above with shining stalactites.

It was a strange enough procession which he followed. But the strangest part of it was the household animals which crowded in around the feet of the goblins. It was true that there were no wild animals down there—at least the goblins did not know of any, but they had a wonderful number of tame ones.

At length, turning a corner too abruptly, Curdie almost rushed headlong into the midst of the goblin family who had set all of their burdens down on the floor of a cave considerably larger than the one they had left. They were as yet too breathless to speak, else he would have had warning of their arrest. He started back before anyone saw him and retreated a good way back, watching until the father should leave to go to the palace.

Before very long, both the father and his son Helfer appeared and kept on in the same direction as before, while Curdie followed them again with renewed precaution. For a long time he heard no sound except something like the rush of a river inside the rock. But at length the far-off noise of great shouting reached his ears and then ceased. After advancing a good way farther, he thought he heard a single voice. It sounded clearer and clearer as he continued, until at last he could almost distinguish the words. He followed the goblins around another corner and started back once more—this time in amazement.

He was at the entrance of a magnificent cavern, oval in shape. It was once probably a huge natural reservoir of water, but was now the great palace hall of the goblins. It rose to a tremendous height with the roof composed of shining materials. The multitude of torches carried by the goblins who crowded the floor lighted up the place so brilliantly that Curdie could see to the top quite well. But he had no idea how immense the place was until his eyes had got accustomed to it, which was not for a good many minutes.

The rough projections on the walls, and the shadows thrown upwards from them by the torches, made the sides of the chamber look as if they were crowded with statues upon brackets and pedestals, reaching in irregular tiers from floor to roof. The walls themselves were, in many parts, of gloriously shining substances, some of them gorgeously colored besides, which powerfully contrasted with the shadows.

Curdie could not help wondering whether his rhymes would be of any use against such a multitude of goblins as filled the floor of the hall, and indeed felt considerably tempted to begin his shout of *One, two, three!*, but there was no reason for routing them before endeavoring to discover their designs. He kept himself perfectly quiet and peered around the edge of the doorway, listening with both his sharp ears.

At the other end of the hall, high above the heads of the multitude, was a terrace-like ledge of considerable height set in the upper part of the cavern wall. Upon this sat the king and his court. The king was on a throne hollowed out of a huge block of green copper ore, and his court was seated below him. The king had been delivering a speech, and it was the applause which followed that Curdie had heard.

One of the court was now pompously addressing the multitude. "Hence it appears that two plans have been for some time together working in the strong head of His Majesty for the deliverance of his people. Regardless of the fact that we were the first possessors of the regions above that they now inhabit; regardless equally of the fact that we abandoned that region from the loftiest motives; regardless also of the self-evident fact that we excel them so far in mental ability as they excel us in stature, they look upon us as a degraded race and make a mockery of all our finer feelings. But the time has almost arrived when—thanks to His Majesty's inventive genius—it will be in our power to take a thorough revenge upon them once for all, in respect of their unfriendly behavior."

"May it please Your Majesty—" cried a voice close by the door. Curdie recognized it as that of the goblin he had followed.

"Who is he that interrupts the chancellor?" cried another from near the throne.

"Glump," answered several voices.

"He is our trusty subject," said the king himself in a slow and stately voice. "Let him come forward and speak."

A lane was parted through the crowd, and Glump passed through, ascended the platform, and bowed to the king.

"Sire, I would have held my peace, except that I know how near is the moment to which the chancellor has just referred. In all probability, before another day is past, the enemy will have broken through into my house—the partition between being even now not more than a foot in thickness."

*Not quite so much,* thought Curdie to himself.

"This very evening I have had to remove my household effects. Therefore, the sooner we are ready to carry out the plan, for which His Majesty has been making such magnificent preparations, the better. I may add, that within the last few days I have perceived a small outbreak in my dining room, which, combined with observations upon the course of the river escaping where the evil men enter, has convinced me that close to the spot must be a deep gulf in its channel. This discovery will, I trust, add considerably to the otherwise immense forces at His Majesty's disposal."

He ceased, and the king graciously acknowledged his speech with a bend of his head. Thereupon Glump, after a bow to His Majesty, slid down amongst the rest of the undistinguished multitude, and then the chancellor rose and resumed.

"The information which the worthy Glump has given us," he said, "might have been of considerable importance at the present moment, but for that other plan already referred to, which naturally takes precedence. His Majesty, unwilling to proceed to extremities, and well aware that such measures sooner or later result in violent reactions, has excogitated a more fundamental and comprehensive measure, of which I need say no more. Should His Majesty be successful—and who would dare to doubt this?—then a peace, all to the advantage of the goblin kingdom, will be established for a generation at least, rendered absolutely secure by the pledge which His Royal Highness the prince will have and hold for the good behavior of her relatives. Should His Majesty fail—which who shall dare even to imagine in his most secret thoughts?—then will be the time for carrying out with rigor the design to which Glump referred, and for which our preparations are even now all but completed. The failure of the former will render the latter imperative."

Curdie perceived that the assembly was drawing to a close and that there was little chance of either plan being more fully discovered. He thought it prudent now to make his escape before the goblins began to disperse, and he slipped quietly away.

There was not much danger of meeting any goblins, for all the men at least were left behind him in the palace. But there was considerable danger of his taking a wrong turn since he had now no light, and had therefore to depend upon his memory.

He was most anxious to get back through the hole before the goblins should return to fetch the remains of their furniture. It was not that he was in the least afraid of them, but it was of the utmost importance that he should discover what the plans were. He must not give them the slightest suspicion that they were watched by a miner.

He hurried on, feeling his way along the walls of rock. Had he not been very courageous, he would have been very anxious, for he knew that if he lost his way it would be the most difficult thing in the world to find again. Morning would bring no light into these regions. And the goblins could not be expected to exercise courtesy towards him, who was known as a harmful rhymester. He wished that he had brought his lamp and tinderbox with him when he crept so eagerly after the goblins, and wished it all the more when he found his way blocked up and could get no farther. It was of no use to turn back, for he had not the least idea where he had begun to go wrong.

Mechanically, however, he kept feeling about the walls that hemmed him in. His hand came upon a place where a tiny stream of water was running down the face of the rock.

"What a stupid I am!" he said to himself. "I am actually at the end of my journey! And there are the goblins coming back to fetch their things!" he added, as the red glimmer of their torches appeared at the end of the long avenue that led up to the cave. In only a moment he had thrown himself on the floor, and wriggled backwards through the hole. The floor on the other side was several feet lower, which made it easier. It was all he could do to lift the largest stone he had taken out of the hole, but he did manage to shove it in again. And then he sat down on the ore-heap and thought.

He was quite sure that the latter plan of the goblins was to flood the mine by breaking outlets into the water accumulated in the natural reservoirs of the mountain. Since the part hollowed by the miners remained as yet shut off from the part inhabited by the goblins, the cobs had no opportunity of injuring them thus far. But now that a passage was broken through, and the goblins' part proved the higher in the mountain, it was clear to Curdie that the mine could be destroyed in an hour.

Water was always the chief danger to which the miners were exposed. Hence they were careful as soon as they saw any appearance of water. As the result of Curdie's reflections while the goblins were busy in their old home, it seemed to him that it would be best to build up this entire gang, filling it with stone and clay so that there would be not even the smallest channel for the water to get into. There was not any immediate danger since the execution of the goblins' plan was contingent upon the failure of the unknown design which was to take place first, and he was eager to keep the door of communication open to discover if possible what the former plan was. They could not resume their intermittent labors for the inundation without his finding it out. If the miners put all their hands to the work, the one existing outlet might in a single night be rendered impenetrable to any weight of water, for by filling the gang entirely up, their embankment would be buttressed by the sides of the mountain itself.

As soon as Curdie found that the goblins had again retired, he lighted his lamp and proceeded to fill the hole he had made with stones that he could withdraw when he pleased. Then, knowing that he might have occasion to be up a good many nights after this, Curdie thought it wise to go home and have some sleep.

How pleasant the night air felt upon the outside of the mountain. He hurried up the hill without meeting a single goblin on the way, and called and tapped at the window until he woke his father, who soon rose and let him in. Curdie told his father the whole story. Just as he had expected, his father thought it best to work that lode no farther, but at the same time to pretend occasionally to be at work there still in order that the goblins might have no suspicions.

# 10

# The Princess's King-Papa

T he weather continued fine for weeks, and the little princess went out every day. So long a period of fine weather had indeed never been known upon that mountain. The only uncomfortable thing was that Nurse was so nervous and particular about being in before the sun was down that often she would take to her heels when nothing worse than a fleecy cloud crossing the sun threw a shadow on the hillside. Many an evening Nurse brought her home a full hour before the sunlight had left the weathervane on the stables. If it had not been for this odd behavior, Irene would have almost forgotten the goblins. She never forgot Curdie, but him she remembered for his own sake.

One splendid sunshiny day, about an hour after noon, Irene was playing on a lawn in the garden and heard the distant blast of a bugle. She jumped up with a cry of joy, for she knew by that particular blast that her father was on his way to see her. This part of the garden lay on the slope of the hill and allowed a full view of the country below. So she shaded her eyes with her hand and looked far away to catch the first glimpse of shining armor. In a few moments a little troop came around the shoulder of a hill. Spears and helmets were sparkling and gleaming, banners were flying, horses prancing, and again came the bugle blast which was to her like the voice of her father calling across the distance: "Irene, I'm coming."

On and on they came until she could clearly distinguish the king. He rode a white horse and was taller than any of the men with him. He wore a narrow circle of gold set with jewels around his helmet, and as he came still nearer Irene could see the flashing of the stones in the sun. It was a long time since he had been to see her, and her heart beat faster and faster as the shining troop approached for she loved her king-papa dearly. When they reached a certain point, she could see them no more from the garden, so she ran to the gate and stood there till up they came, clanging and stamping, with one more bright bugle blast which declared: "Irene, I am come."

By this time all the people of the house were gathered at the gate, but Irene stood alone in front of them. When the horsemen pulled up, she ran to the side of the white horse and held up her arms. The king stopped and took her hands. In an instant she was on the saddle and clasped in his great strong arms.

The king had gentle, blue eyes, but a nose that made him look like an eagle. A long dark beard, streaked with silvery lines, flowed from his mouth almost to his waist, and Irene leaned against him so that her golden hair mingled with his beard. The two together were like a cloud with streaks of the sun woven through it.

After he had held her tightly to his heart for a minute, he spoke to his white horse, and the great beautiful creature, which had been prancing so proudly a little while before, walked as gently as a lady through the gate and up to the door of the house, for he knew he had the princess on his back. Then the king set Irene on the ground and, dismounting, took her hand and walked with her into the great hall—a hall scarcely ever entered except when he came to see his little princess. There he sat down to have some refreshment with two of his counselors who had accompanied him. Irene sat on his right hand and drank her milk out of a curiously carved wooden bowl.

After the king had eaten, he turned to the princess, stroked her hair, and said, "Now, my child, what shall we do next?"

This was the question he almost always put to her first after their meal together, and Irene had been waiting for it with some impatience. For now she thought she would be able to settle a question which constantly perplexed her.

"I would like you to take me to see my old great-great-grandmother."

The king looked grave and said, "What does my little daughter mean?"

"I mean the Queen Irene that lives up in the tower. You know. The very old lady with the long hair of silver."

The king only gazed at his little princess with a look which she could not understand.

"She's got her crown in her bedroom," Irene went on, "but I've not been in there yet. You know she's there, don't you?"

"No," said the king very quietly.

"Then it *must* all be a dream," said Irene. "I half thought it was, but I couldn't be sure. Now I am. Besides, I couldn't find her the next time I went up."

At that moment a snow white pigeon flew in at an open window and settled upon Irene's head. She broke into a merry laugh and put up her hands to her head.

The king stretched out his hand to take the pigeon, but it spread its wings and flew again through the open window, where its whiteness made one flash in the sun and vanished. The king laid his hand on his princess's head, held it back a little, and gazed into her face. He smiled half a smile and sighed half a sigh.

"Come, my child. We'll have a walk in the garden together," he said.

"You won't come up and see my beautiful great-great-grandmother, then, King-Papa?" said the princess.

"Not this time," said the king very gently. "She has not invited me, you know. And great old ladies like her do not choose to be visited without permission asked and given."

The garden was a very lovely place. Being upon a mountainside there were parts in it where the rocks came through in great masses and all immediately about them remained quite wild. Tufts of heather grew upon them, and other hardy mountain plants and flowers, while near them would be lovely roses and lilies and all pleasant garden flowers. This mingling of the wild mountain with the civilized garden was very quaint, and it was impossible for any number of gardeners to make such a garden look formal and stiff.

Against one of these rocks was a garden seat, shadowed from the afternoon sun by the overhang of the rock itself. They sat on the seat and there they talked together of many things.

At length the king said, "You were out late one evening, Irene."

"Yes, Papa. It was my fault, and Lootie was very sorry."

"I must talk to Lootie about it," said the king.

"Don't let her go, please, Papa," said Irene. "She's been so afraid of being late ever since! Indeed she has not been naughty. It was only a mistake for once."

"Once might be too often," murmured the king to himself, as he stroked his child's head.

Irene did not know how he had come to know. Curdie could not have told him, so someone about the palace must have seen them after all.

The king sat for a good while thinking. There was no sound to be heard except that of a little stream which ran out of an opening in the rock near where they sat, then trickled away down the hill through the garden.

At long last the king arose, and, leaving Irene where she was, he went into the house and sent for Lootie with whom he had a talk that made her cry.

When in the evening he rode away upon his great white horse, he left six of his attendants behind him, with orders that three of them should watch outside the house every night, walking round and round it from sunset to sunrise.

It was clear he was not quite comfortable about the princess.

# 11

# The Old Lady's Bedroom

Nothing more happened for some time. The autumn came and went. The wind blew strong and howled among the rocks. The rain fell and drenched the few yellow and red leaves that could not yet get off the bare branches. Again and again there would be a glorious morning followed by a pouring afternoon. And sometimes for a week altogether, there would be rain, nothing but rain, all day. This would be followed by the loveliest cloudless night filled with stars, and not one missing.

But the princess could not see them, for she went to bed early. The winter drew on, and she found things growing dreary. When it was too stormy to go out, and she had got tired of her toys, Lootie would take her about the house. Sometimes they went to the housekeeper's room, where the housekeeper, who was a good, kind old woman, made much of her. Sometimes they went to the servants' hall or the kitchen, where she was not merely princess, but absolute queen, and ran a great risk of being spoiled. Sometimes she would run off by herself to the room where the men-at-arms whom the king had left sat. They showed her their arms and accoutrements and did what they could to amuse her. And often and often there were times she wished that her huge great-grandmother had not been a dream.

One morning Nurse left her with the housekeeper for a while, who turned out the contents of an old cabinet upon the table to amuse the princess. Irene found the housekeeper's treasures, queer ancient ornaments and many things the use of which she could not imagine, far more interesting than her own toys, and sat playing with them for two hours or more. But, at length, in handling a curious old-fashioned brooch, she ran the pin of it into her thumb and gave a little cry at the sharpness of the pain. She would have thought little more of it had not the pain increased and her thumb begun to swell. This alarmed the housekeeper greatly. The nurse was fetched; the doctor was sent for; her hand was poulticed, and long before her usual time she was put to bed. The pain continued still, and although she fell asleep and dreamed a good many dreams, there was the pain always in every dream. At last it woke her up.

The moon was shining brightly into the room. The poultice had fallen off her hand, and it was burning hot. She fancied that if she could hold her hand in the moonlight it would cool, so she got out of bed without waking Nurse, who lay at the other end of the room, and went to the window. When she looked out, she saw one of the men-at-arms walking in the garden with the moonlight glancing on his armor. She was going to tap on the window and call to him, for she wanted to tell him all about it. But she thought to herself that it might wake Lootie who would just put her to bed again. So she resolved to go to the window of another room and call to him from there.

It would be much nicer to have somebody to talk to rather than to lie awake in bed with the burning pain in her hand. She opened the door very gently and went through the nursery to go to the other window. But when she came to the foot of the old staircase, there was the moon shining down from some window high up, making the worm-eaten oak look very strange and delicate and lovely. In a moment she was putting her little feet one after the other in the silvery path up the stair, looking behind as she went, to see the shadow she made in the middle of the silver. Princess Irene was not afraid.

As she went slowly up the stair, not quite sure that she was not dreaming, she suddenly had a great longing to try once more to find the old lady with the silvery hair. "If she is a dream," she said to herself, "then I am the likelier to find her, if I am dreaming."

So up and up she went, stair after stair, until she came to the many rooms—all just as she had seen them before. Through passage after passage she went softly, comforting herself that if she should lose her way it would not matter much, because when she woke she would find herself in her own bed with Lootie not far off. But it was almost as if she had known every step of the way, for she walked straight to the door at the foot of the narrow stair that led to the tower.

"What if I should really find my beautiful old great-great-grandmother up there?" she said to herself as she crept up the steep steps.

When she reached the top, she stood a moment listening in the dark, for there was no moon there. Yes! It was the hum of the spinning wheel. What a diligent grandmother to work both day and night. She tapped gently at the door.

"Come in, Irene," said the sweet voice.

The princess opened the door and entered. There was the moonlight streaming in at the window, and in the middle of the moonlight sat the old lady in her black dress with the white lace, and her silvery hair mingling with the moonlight.

"Come in, Irene," she said again. "Can you tell me what I am spinning?"

*She speaks,* thought Irene, *just as if she had seen me five minutes ago, or yesterday at the farthest.*

"No," Irene answered. "I don't know what you are spinning. Please, I thought you were a dream. Why couldn't I find you before, great-great-grandmother?"

"That you are hardly old enough to understand. But you would have found me sooner if you hadn't come to think I was a dream. I will give you one reason though why you couldn't find me. I didn't want you to find me."

"Why, please?"

"Because I did not want Nurse to know I was here."

"But you told me to tell Nurse."

"Yes. But I knew Nurse would not believe you. If she were to see me sitting spinning here, she wouldn't believe me either."

"Why?"

"Because she couldn't. She would rub her eyes, and go away. She would forget half of it and more, and then say it had been all a dream."

"Just like me," said Irene, feeling very much ashamed.

"Yes, a good deal like you, but not *just* like you; for you have come again. Nurse wouldn't have come again."

"Is it naughty of Nurse then?"

"It would be naughty of you, but I have never done anything for Nurse."

"And you did wash my face and hands for me," said Irene.

The old lady smiled a sweet smile and said, "I'm not vexed with you, my child—nor with Nurse. But I don't want you to say anything more to Nurse about me. I do not think she will ask you, but if she does, you must just be silent."

All the time they talked the old lady kept on spinning.

"You haven't told me yet what I am spinning," she said.

"Because I don't know. It's very pretty."

It was indeed very pretty. There was a good bunch of it on the distaff attached to the spinning wheel, and in the moonlight it shone like silver. The thread the old lady drew out from it was so fine that Irene could hardly see it.

"I am spinning this for you, my child."

"What am I to do with it, please?"

"I will tell you by and by. But first I will tell you what it is. It is spider web—of a particular kind. My pigeons bring it to me from over the great sea. There is only one forest where the spiders live who make this particular kind—the finest and strongest. I have nearly finished this. What is on the rock now will be enough," she added, looking at the bunch.

"Do you work all day and all night too, great-great-great-great-grandmother?" said the princess, thinking to be very polite with so many greats.

"I am not quite so great as all that," she answered, smiling almost merrily. "If you call me grandmother, that will do. No, I don't work every night—only moonlit nights, and then no longer than the moon shines upon my wheel. I shan't work much longer tonight."

"And what will you do next, Grandmother?"

"Go to bed. Would you like to see my bedroom?"

"Yes, I would."

"Then I think I won't work any longer tonight."

The old lady rose and left her wheel standing just as it was. There was no use in putting it away, for there was not any other furniture and so no danger of being untidy.

Then the grandmother took Irene by the hand. But it was her bad hand, and Irene gave a little cry of pain.

"My child!" said her grandmother, "what is the matter?"

Irene held her hand into the moonlight so that the old lady might see it, and told her all about it. The old lady looked grave, but said only, "Give me your other hand."

She led Irene out onto the little dark landing and opened the door on the opposite side of it. Irene was surprised to see the loveliest room she had ever seen in her life. It was large and lofty and dome-shaped. From the center hung a lamp as round as a ball, shining as if with the brightest moonlight. It made everything visible in the room, though not so clearly that the princess could tell what many of the things were. A large oval bed stood in the middle with a cover of rose color, and velvet curtains all around of a lovely pale blue. The walls were also blue and spangled all over with what looked like stars of silver.

The old lady left her and went to a strange-looking cabinet, opened it, and took out a curious silver casket. Then she sat down on a low chair and, calling Irene, made her kneel before her while she looked at her hand. Having examined it, she opened the casket and took from it a little ointment. The sweetest odor filled the room as she rubbed the ointment gently all over the hot swollen hand. Her touch was so pleasant and cool that it seemed to drive away the pain and heat wherever it came.

"Oh, Grandmother, that is so nice!" said Irene. "Thank you, thank you."

Then the old lady went to a chest of drawers and took out a large handkerchief of delicate linen, which she tied around Irene's hand.

"I don't think I can let you go away tonight," she said. "Would you like to sleep with me?"

"Oh, yes, dear Grandmother," said Irene. She would have clapped her hands, but remembered that she could not.

"You won't be afraid then, to go to bed with such an old woman?"

"No. You are so beautiful, Grandmother."

"But I am very old."

"And I suppose I am very young. You won't mind sleeping with such a very young woman, Grandmother?"

The old lady drew Irene towards her and kissed her on the forehead and both of her cheeks. Then she got a large silver basin, and having poured some water into it made Irene sit on the chair, and washed her feet. This done, she was ready for bed.

Oh, what a delicious bed it was into which her grandmother laid her! She hardly could have told she was lying upon anything for she felt nothing but softness.

The old lady herself lay down beside her.

"Why don't you put out your moon?" asked the princess.

"That never goes out, night or day," she answered. "In the darkest night, if any of my pigeons are out on a message, they always see my moon and know where to fly to."

"But if somebody besides the pigeons were to see it—somebody from the house, I mean—they would come to look what it was and find you."

"The better for them, then," said the old lady. "But it does not happen five times in a hundred years that anyone does see it. Most of those who do take it for a meteor, wink their eyes, and forget it again. And I will tell you a secret—if that light were to go out, you would fancy yourself lying in a bare garret, on a heap of old straw, and would not see one of the pleasant things round about you all the time."

"Then I hope it will never go out," said the princess.

"I hope not. But it is time we both went to sleep."

The little princess nestled close up to the old lady, who took her in both her arms and held her close.

"I didn't know anything in the world could be so comfortable," said the princess. "I should like to lie here for ever."

"You may if you wish," said the old lady. "But I must put you to one trial—not a very hard one, I hope. In one week you must come back to me. If you don't, I do not know when you may find me again, and you will soon want me very much."

"Oh! please, don't let me forget."

"You shall not forget. The only question is whether you will believe I am anywhere—whether you will believe I am anything but a dream. You may be sure I will do all I can to help you to come. But it will rest with you. On the night of next Friday, you must come to me. Mind now."

"I will try," said the princess.

"Then good night," said the old lady and kissed the forehead which lay beside her.

In a moment the little princess was dreaming the loveliest dreams—of summer seas and moonlight and mossy springs and great murmuring trees and beds of wild flowers with such odors as she had never smelled before. But no dream could be lovelier than what she had left behind when she fell asleep.

In the morning she found herself in her own bed. There was no handkerchief or anything else on her hand, only a lingering sweet odor. The swelling had all gone down; the prick of the brooch had vanished. In fact, her hand was perfectly well.

# 12

# A Short Chapter
# about Curdie

Curdie spent many nights in the mine. His father and he had let Mrs. Peterson in on the secret. They knew Mother could hold her tongue, which was more than could be said of all the miners' wives.

But Curdie did not tell her that for every night he spent in the mine, part of it went to earning a new red petticoat for her.

Mrs. Peterson was such a nice good mother. All mothers are nice and good more or less, but Mrs. Peterson was nice and good all more and no less. She made and kept a little heaven in that poor cottage on the high hillside for her husband and son to go home to. True, her hands were hard and chapped and large, but it was because of her work for them. That made her hands so much the more beautiful. And if Curdie worked hard to get her a petticoat, she worked hard every day to get him comforts which he would have missed much more than she would a new petticoat even in winter. Not that she and

Curdie ever thought of how much they worked for each other, for that would have spoiled everything.

When left alone in the mine Curdie always worked on for an hour or two, at first following the lode which Glump had said would lead into his deserted habitation. After that, Curdie set out on a reconnoitering expedition. In order to manage returning from each survey better than the first time, he had bought a huge ball of fine string. The end of this string he fastened to his pickaxe, which served as an anchor. And then, with the ball in his hand, unrolling it as he went, he set out in the dark through the natural gangs of the goblins' territory.

The first night or two he came upon nothing worth remembering. He saw only a little of the home life of the cobs in the various caves they called houses. He failed to come upon anything to cast light on the forthcoming plot which kept the flood in the background for now. But at length he found, partly guided by the noise of their implements, a company of evidently the best sappers and miners amongst them, hard at work. What were they about? It could not well be the inundation, seeing that had been postponed for the present time. But what was it?

He lurked and watched at the greatest risk of being detected, but without success. He retreated in haste again and again, a proceeding rendered the more difficult since he had to gather up his string as he returned upon its course. It was not that he was afraid of the goblins, but that he was afraid of their finding out that they were watched. Sometimes his haste had to be such that his string would be hopelessly entangled

when he reached home in the morning since he had no time
to wind it up as he dodged the cobs. But after a good sleep,
even a short one, he always found his mother had set it right
again. There it was, wound in a most respectable ball, ready
for use the next moment he should want it.

"I can't think how you do it, Mother," he would say.

"I follow the thread," she would answer, "just as you do
in the mine." She never had more to say about it; but the less
clever she was with her words, the more clever she was with
her hands. And the less his mother said, the more Curdie believed what she had to say.

But still he had made no discovery as to what the goblin
miners were about.

## 13

# THE COBS' CREATURES

At about this time the gentlemen whom the king had left behind to watch over the princess had each occasion to doubt the testimony of his own eyes. Each saw objects more strange than they could describe. They were of one sort—creatures—but so grotesque and misshapen as to be more like a child's drawings upon a slate than anything natural. The men-at-arms saw them only at night while on guard about the house.

The testimony of the first man who reported having seen one of them was this: as he was walking slowly in the shadows around the house, he caught sight in the moonlight of a creature standing on its hind legs with its forefeet upon a window ledge and staring in at the window. Its body might have been that of a dog or wolf, he thought, but he declared on his honor that its head was twice the size it ought to have been for the size of its body. The head was as round as a ball, while the face was more like one carved on the side of a turnip inside which a candle will be lit. The creature rushed into the garden. The guard sent an arrow after it, and thought he must have struck it, for it gave an unearthly howl. Yet he could not find his arrow any more than the beast, although he searched all about the place where it vanished. The other men laughed at him until he was driven to hold his tongue.

But before two nights were over he had one to side with him, for another man too had seen something strange, only quite different from that reported by the first.

The description the second man gave of the creature he had seen was yet more grotesque and unbelievable. Both men were laughed at by the rest. But night after night others came over to their side, until at last there was only one man left to laugh at all his companions.

Two nights more passed, and he saw nothing. But on the third he came rushing from the garden in such agitation that the other two guards declared—for it was their turn now— that the band of his helmet was cracking under his chin with the rising of his hair inside it.

They ran back with him into the garden where they saw a score of creatures. They could not give a name to any one of them, nor was one of them like another. They were each hideous and ludicrous at once, gamboling on the lawn in the moonlight. The unnatural ugliness of their faces, the length of legs and necks in some, the apparent absence of both or either in others, made the spectators doubtful, although in one consent as to what they saw. Keeping in the shadows, the watchers had a few moments to recover themselves before the hideous assembly suspected their presence, and all at once, as if by common consent, scampered off in the direction of a great rock. They vanished before the men had come to themselves sufficiently to think of following them.

The creatures were, of course, household animals belonging to the goblins.

Curdie had discovered that the goblins were mining on both day and night. In the course of their tunneling, they had broken into the channel of a small stream; but the break being near the top of it, no water had escaped to interfere with their work. The stream was the same which ran out by the seat on which Irene and her king-papa had sat where the goblin's creatures found it great fun to romp on a smooth lawn such as they had never seen in all their poor miserable lives. And they had enough of the nature of their owners to delight in annoying and alarming any people whom they met on the mountain.

For several nights after the men-at-arms were at last of one mind as to the fact of the horrible creatures, they carefully watched that part of the garden where they had last seen them. Perhaps in consequence they gave too little attention to the house, but the creatures were too cunning to be easily caught.

## 14

# THAT NIGHT WEEK

During the whole week Irene had been thinking every other moment of her promise to the old lady, although even now she could not feel quite certain that she had not been dreaming. Could it really be that an old lady lived up in the top of the house with pigeons and a spinning wheel and a lamp that never went out? The princess was nonetheless determined to ascend the three stairs on the coming Friday, to walk through the passages with the many doors, and to try to find the tower in which she had either seen or dreamed her grandmother.

Nurse could not help wondering what had come over the child. She would sit so thoughtfully silent, and even in the midst of a game would suddenly fall into a dreamy mood. But Irene took care to betray nothing, whatever efforts Lootie might make to get at her thoughts.

At length the longed-for Friday arrived, and Irene endeavored to keep herself as quiet as possible lest Lootie should suspect anything. In the afternoon Irene asked for her doll's house, and arranged and rearranged the various rooms and their inhabitants for a whole hour. Then she gave a sigh and threw herself back in her chair. One of the dolls would not sit, and another would not stand, and they were all very tiresome. Indeed, there was one would not even lie down, which was too bad.

But it was now getting dark, and the darker it got, the more excited Irene became. And the more she felt it necessary to be composed.

"I see you are ready for your tea, Princess," said Nurse. "I will go and get it. The room feels close. I will open the window a little first. The evening is mild, so it won't hurt you."

"There's no fear of that, Lootie," said Irene, wishing she had put off going for the tea till it was darker still, when she might have made her attempt with every advantage.

Lootie was longer in returning than she had intended, and Irene, who had been lost in thought, looked up and saw it was nearly dark. At the same moment she caught sight of a pair of eyes, bright with a green light, glowering at her through the open window. The next instant something leaped into the room. It was like a cat with legs as long as a horse's, but its body no bigger and its legs no thicker than those of a cat. Irene was too frightened to cry out, but not too frightened to jump from her chair and run from the room.

Irene thought of what she ought to have done, but when she came to the foot of the old stair just outside the nursery door, she imagined the creature running after her up those long ascents, pursuing her through the dark passages. Passages which might, after all, lead to no tower at all! That thought was frightening, and Irene's heart failed her. Turning away from the stair, she rushed along to the hall, out the front door and into the court pursued by the creature—or at least so she thought.

No one happened to see her, so on she ran too afraid even to think and ready to run anywhere to elude the awful creature with the stilt legs. Not daring to look behind her, she rushed straight out of the gate and up the mountain. It was foolish indeed to run farther and farther from all who could help her. It was as if she was seeking a fit spot for the goblin creature to eat her at his leisure. But that is the way fear served her, siding with the thing she was most afraid of.

The princess was running out of breath, but she ran on, for she fancied the horrible creature just behind her. She failed to think that if it had been chasing her on such long legs, it would have overtaken her long ago. At last she could run no longer and fell by the roadside, unable even to scream. She lay there for some time half dead with terror, but as nothing lay hold of her and her breath was beginning to come back, she ventured at length to get half up and peer anxiously about her. It was now so dark she could see nothing. Not a single star was out. She could not even tell in what direction the house lay, and between her and home she fancied the dreadful creature lying ready to pounce upon her.

She knew now that she ought to have run up the stairs at once. She had quite forgotten her promise to visit her grandmother. She sat down upon a stone, and nobody but one who had done something terribly wrong could have been more miserable. A raindrop fell on her face, and she looked up. For a moment her terror was lost in astonishment. At first she thought the rising moon had left its place and drawn nigh to see what could be the matter with the girl sitting alone without hat or cloak on the dark bare mountain. But she soon saw that she was mistaken, for there was no light shining on the ground at her feet, and no shadow anywhere. And yet the great silver globe was hanging in the air, and as Irene gazed at the lovely thing, her courage revived.

If she were but indoors again, she would fear nothing, not even the terrible creature with the long legs. But how was she to find her way back? What could that light be? Could it be—? No, it couldn't. But what if it should be . . . yes . . . it must be her great-great-grandmother's lamp, which guided her pigeons home through the darkest night! She jumped up knowing that she had but to keep that light in view and she would find the house. Her heart grew strong. Speedily, yet softly, she walked down the hill, hoping to pass the watching creature unseen.

Dark as it was, there was little danger now of choosing the wrong road. And strangely enough, the light that filled her eyes from the lamp, instead of blinding them for a moment, enabled her to see the object upon which they next fell despite the darkness. By looking at the lamp and then dropping her eyes, she could see the rough road for a yard or two in front of her, and this saved her from several falls. And then to her dismay, the light vanished, and the terror of the beast again laid hold of her heart.

The same instant, however, she caught the light of the windows and knew exactly where she was. It was too dark to run, but she made what haste she could and reached the gate in safety. She found the door to the house still open, ran through the hall, and, without even looking into the nursery, bounded straight up one stair, and the next, and the next. Then turning to the right through the long avenue of silent rooms, she found her way to the door at the foot of the tower stair.

When first Nurse missed her, she fancied Irene was playing a trick on her, and so for some time gave it no thought. But frightened at last, she had begun to search. When the princess entered, the whole household was hither and thither over the house, hunting for her. A few seconds after she reached the stair of the tower they had even begun to search the neglected rooms in which they would never have thought of looking had they not already searched every other place they could think of in vain.

But by this time she was knocking at the old lady's door.

## 15

# WOVEN AND THEN SPUN

"Come in, Irene," said the silvery voice of her grandmother.

The princess opened the door and peeped in, but the room was quite dark. She remembered that the old lady said she spun only in the moonlight, and since Irene heard no sweet, bee-like humming of the spinning wheel, she knew that the grandmother was not spinning. She might be somewhere in the darkness, but perhaps even though the room was there, the old lady might be a dream after all.

Before the princess had time to think another thought, she heard the voice again, saying as before, "Come in, Irene."

From the sound, she understood at once that the lady was not in the room beside her, and so she turned across the passage, feeling for the other door. When her hand fell on the lock, again the old lady spoke. "Shut the other door behind you, Irene. I always close the door of my workroom when I go to my chamber."

Irene was surprised to hear the voice so plainly through the door. She shut the first door, and then opened the chamber and went in. It was a lovely haven from the darkness and fear through which she had come. The soft light made her feel as if she were going into the heart of the milkiest pearl, while the blue walls and their silver stars for a moment perplexed her with the thought that they were in reality the sky she had left outside only a minute ago covered with rain clouds.

"I've lit a fire for you, Irene. You're cold and wet," said her grandmother.

Then Irene looked again and saw that what she had taken for a huge bouquet of red roses on a low stand against the wall was in fact a fire which burned in the shapes of the loveliest and reddest roses. It glowed brightly between the heads and wings of two cherubs of shining silver, and the smell of roses filled the room. Her grandmother was dressed in lovely pale blue velvet, over which her hair fell smoothly. It was no longer white, but a rich golden color, and it flowed from under the edge of a shining band of silver, set with pearls and opals. On her dress was no ornament whatever; no ring on her hand; no necklace about her neck. But her slippers were covered with seed pearls and opals in one mass, and they glimmered with the light of the Milky Way. Her face was that of a woman of three-and-twenty.

The princess was so bewildered with astonishment and admiration that she timidly drew nigh, feeling dirty and uncomfortable. The lady was seated on a low chair by the side of the fire. Her hands were outstretched, but the princess hung back with a troubled smile.

"Why, what's the matter?" asked her grandmother. "You haven't been doing anything wrong—I know that by your face, though it is rather miserable. What's the matter, my dear?"

And she still held out her arms.

"Dear Grandmother," said Irene, "I'm not so sure that I've done nothing wrong. I ought to have run up to you at once when the long-legged cat came in at the window. But instead I ran out on the mountain and made myself such a fright."

"You were taken by surprise, my child, and you are not so likely to do so again. It is when people do wrong things willfully that they are the more likely to do them again. Come."

And still she held out her arms.

"But, Grandmother, you're so beautiful and grand with your crown on. I am so dirty with mud and rain. I will spoil your beautiful blue dress."

With a merry little laugh the lady sprung from her chair, pulled the child to herself, and kissing the tear-stained face, sat down with her in her lap.

"Oh, Grandmother! You'll make yourself such a mess!" cried Irene, yet clinging to her.

"Dear girl. Do you think I care more for my dress than for you? Besides—look here."

As she spoke, she set Irene down, who saw to her dismay that the lovely dress was covered with mud from her fall on the mountain road. But the lady stooped to the fire, took from it one of the burning roses, and passed it once and again and a third time over the front of her dress. When Irene looked, not a single stain was to be discovered.

"There!" said her grandmother, "you won't mind coming to me now?"

But Irene again hung back, eyeing the flaming rose which the lady held in her hand.

"You're not afraid of the rose. Are you?" she said, about to throw it on the hearth again.

"Oh, please!" cried Irene. "Won't you hold it to my frock and my hands and my face? And I'm afraid my feet and my knees need it too."

"No," answered her grandmother, smiling a little sadly, as she threw the rose from her, "it is too hot for you yet. It would set your frock in a flame. Besides, I don't want to make you clean tonight. I want your nurse and the rest of the people to see you as you are, for you will have to tell them how you ran away for fear of the long-legged cat. I would like to wash you, but they would not believe you then. Do you see that bath behind you?"

The princess looked, and saw a large oval tub of silver, shining brilliantly in the light of the wonderful lamp.

"Go and look into it," said the lady.

Irene went and came back silently with her eyes shining.

"What did you see?"

"The sky, and the moon, and the stars," she answered. "It looked as if there was no bottom to it."

The lady smiled a pleased, satisfied smile and was also silent for a few moments. Then she said, "Any time you want a bath, come to me. I know you have a bath every morning, but sometimes you may want one at night too."

"Thank you, Grandmother. I will. I will indeed," answered Irene, and was again silent for some moments thinking. Then she said, "How was it, Grandmother, that I saw your beautiful lamp—not the light of it only—but the great round silvery lamp itself, hanging alone in the great open air, high up? It was your lamp I saw, wasn't it?"

"Yes, my child. It was my lamp."

"Then how was it? I don't see a window anywhere."

"When I please, I can make the lamp shine through the walls—shine so strong that it melts them away from before the sight, and shows itself as you saw it. But, as I told you, it is not everybody can see it."

"How is it that *I* can, then? I'm sure I don't know."

"It is a gift born with you. And one day I hope everybody will have it."

"But how do you make it shine through the walls?"

"Ah! that you would not understand if I were to try ever so much to make you. Not yet . . . not yet. But," added the lady, rising, "you must sit in my chair while I get you the present I have been preparing for you. I told you my spinning was for you. It is finished now, and I am going to fetch it. I have been keeping it warm under one of my brooding pigeons."

Irene sat down in the low chair, and her grandmother left her, shutting the door behind. The child sat gazing first at the rose fire, then at the starry walls, finally at the silver light, and a great quietness grew in her heart. If all the long-legged cats in the world had come rushing at her, she would not have been afraid of them for a moment. She did not know why this was. She only knew there was no fear in her.

When she turned her eyes, she found the wall had vanished, and she was looking out on the dark cloudy night. And though she heard the wind blowing, none of it blew upon her. In a moment more the clouds vanished like the wall, and she looked straight into the starry herds, flashing gloriously in the dark blue—but for a moment. The clouds gathered again and shut out the stars; the wall gathered again and shut out the clouds; and there stood the lady beside her with the loveliest smile on her face, and a shimmering ball in her hand, about the size of a pigeon's egg.

"Here, Irene. Here is my work for you," she said, holding out the ball to the princess.

Irene took it in her hand and looked at it all over. It sparkled a little and shone here and there, but not much. It was of a sort of gray-whiteness, something like spun glass.

"Is this all your spinning, Grandmother?" she asked.

"All since you came to the house. There is more there than you think."

"How pretty it is! What am I to do with it, please?"

"I will explain that to you now," answered the lady, turning from her and going to her cabinet. She came back with a small ring in her hand. She took the ball from Irene and did something with the ring—Irene could not tell what.

"Give me your hand," she said. Irene held up her right hand.

"Yes, that is the hand I want," said the lady, and she put the ring on the forefinger of it.

"What a beautiful ring!" said Irene. "What is the stone called?"

"It is a fire opal."

"Am I to keep it?"

"Always."

"Oh, thank you, Grandmother! It's prettier than anything I ever saw, except for those in your— Please, is that your crown?"

"Yes, it is my crown. The stone in your ring is of the same sort—only not so good. It has only red, but mine have all colors, you see."

"Yes, Grandmother. I will take such care of it! But—" she added, hesitating.

"But what?" asked her grandmother.

"What am I to say when Lootie asks me where I got it?"

"You will ask *her* where you got it," answered the lady, smiling, "For she may remember."

So saying, the lady turned, and threw the little ball into the rose fire.

"Oh, no!" exclaimed Irene. "I thought you had spun it for me."

"So I did, my child. And you've got it."

"No, it's burnt in the fire!"

The lady put her hand into the fire, brought out the ball, glimmering as before, and held it towards her. Irene stretched out her hand to take it, but the lady turned and, going to her cabinet, opened a drawer, and laid the ball in it.

"Have I done anything to vex you, Grandmother?" said Irene pitifully.

"No, my darling. But you must understand that no one ever gives anything to another properly and really without keeping it. That ball is yours."

"I think I see. I'm not to take it with me. You are going to keep it for me?"

"You are to take it with you. I've fastened the end of it to the ring on your finger."

Irene looked at the ring.

"I can't see it," she said.

"Feel—a little way from the ring—towards the cabinet," said the lady.

"Oh! I do feel it!" exclaimed the princess. "But I can't see it," she added, looking close to her outstretched hand.

"No. The thread is too fine for you to see it. You can only feel it. Now you can fancy how much spinning that took, although it does seem such a little ball."

"But what use can I make of it, if it lies in your cabinet?"

"That is what I will explain. Now listen. If ever you find yourself in any danger—such as you were this evening—you must take off your ring and put it under the pillow of your bed. Then you must lay your finger, the same that wore the ring, upon the thread, and follow the thread wherever it leads you."

"How delightful! It will lead me to you, Grandmother, I know!"

"Yes. But, remember, it may seem to you a very roundabout way, and you must not doubt the thread. Of one thing you may be very sure. While you hold the thread, I hold it too."

"It is very wonderful," said Irene thoughtfully. "But won't the thread get in somebody's way and be broken if the one end is fast to my ring and the other laid in your cabinet?"

"You will find that it will arrange itself. It is time for you to go."

"May I stay and sleep with you tonight, Grandmother?"

"No, not tonight. If I had meant for you to stay tonight, I would have given you a bath. But you know everybody in the house is worried about you, and it would be cruel to keep them so all night. You must go downstairs."

"I'm so glad, Grandmother, you didn't say 'Go home,' for this is my home. May I call this my home?"

"You may, my child. And I trust you will always think it your home. Now come. I must take you back without anyone seeing you."

"Please, I want to ask you one question more," said Irene. "Is it because you have your crown on that you look so young?"

"No, child," answered her grandmother. "It is because I felt so young this evening that I put my crown on. And I thought you would like to see your old grandmother in her best."

"You're not old, Grandmother."

"I am very old indeed. It is so silly of people—I don't mean you, for you couldn't know better yet—but it is silly of people to fancy that old age means crookedness and witheredness and feebleness and sticks and spectacles and rheumatism and forgetfulness. Old age has nothing whatever to do with all that. The right old age means strength and beauty and mirth and courage and clear eyes and strong painless limbs. I am older than you are able to think, and—"

"And look at you, Grandmother!" cried Irene, jumping up and flinging her arms about her neck. "I wish I were as old as you, Grandmother. I don't think you are ever afraid of anything."

"Perhaps by the time I am two thousand years of age, I shall never be afraid of anything. But I confess I have sometimes been afraid about my children—sometimes about you, Irene."

"I'm so sorry, Grandmother. Tonight, I suppose you mean."

"Yes—a little tonight; but a good deal more when you had nearly made up your mind that I was a dream, and no real great-great-grandmother. I am not blaming you for that. I dare say you could not help it."

"I can't always do as I should like, Grandmother," said the princess, beginning to cry. "And I don't always try. I'm very sorry anyhow."

The lady stooped, lifted the princess in her arms, and sat down with her in her chair, holding her close. In a few minutes the princess had sobbed herself to sleep.

When she awakened, she was sitting in her own chair at the nursery table with her doll's house before her.

## 16

# THE RING

The very same moment Nurse came into the room; and when she saw Irene sitting there, she started back with a cry of joy. She caught her up in her arms and kissed her.

"My darling princess! Where have you been? We've been searching the house from top to bottom for you."

*Not quite from the top,* thought Irene to herself; and she might have added, *not quite to the bottom,* if she had known all. But the one she *would* not, and the other she *could* not say.

"Oh, Lootie! I've had such a dreadful adventure," she replied and told her all about the cat with the long legs, and how she ran out upon the mountain and came back again. But of her grandmother or her lamp she said nothing at all.

"And here we've been searching for you all over the house for more than an hour and a half!" exclaimed the nurse. "But that's no matter now. Only, Princess," she added, her mood changing, "what you ought to have done was to call for me to come and help you, instead of running out of the house and up the mountain in that wild, foolish fashion."

"Well, Lootie," said Irene quietly, "if you had a big cat, all legs, running at you, you might not exactly know what was the wisest thing to do at the moment either."

"I wouldn't run up the mountain," returned Lootie.

"Not if you had time to think about it. But remember when those creatures came at you that night on the mountain? You were so frightened then that you lost your way home."

This put a stop to Lootie's reproaches. She had nearly said that the long-legged cat must have been a twilight fancy of the princess's, but the memories of the horrors of that night and of the talking-to which the king had given her in consequence were sufficient to prevent her from saying that she did not half believe there was a cat.

Without another word she went and got some fresh tea and bread and butter for the princess. Before she returned, the whole household, headed by the housekeeper, burst into the nursery to fawn over the child. The gentlemen-at-arms followed and were ready enough to believe all she told them about the long-legged cat. Indeed, though wise enough to say nothing about it, they remembered with no small horror just such a creature amongst those they had surprised at their gambols upon the princess's lawn.

In their own hearts they blamed themselves for not having kept better watch. And their captain gave orders that from this night forward the front door and all the windows on the ground floor should be locked immediately upon sunset. They were not to be opened on any pretense whatsoever. The men-at-arms redoubled their vigilance, and for some time there was no further cause for alarm.

When the princess awoke the next morning, Nurse was bending over her. "How your ring does glow this morning, princess! Just like a fiery rose," she said.

"Does it?" returned Irene. "Tell me about the ring, Lootie. Where did I get it?"

"It must have been your mother gave it you, Princess; but really, for as long as you have had it, I don't remember that ever I heard," answered Nurse.

"Was it a gift from my very old great-great-grandmother upstairs?"

"What do you mean by that? You are talking nonsense, Irene."

"Then, Lootie, I will ask my king-papa the next time he comes."

# 17

# SPRINGTIME

The spring came at last, and before the first few days of it were past, the king rode through the budding valleys to see his little daughter. All winter he had been in a distant part of his dominions. He was not in the habit of stopping in one great city or of visiting only his favorite country houses, but rather he moved from place to place so that all his people might know him. He kept a constant lookout for the ablest and best men to put into office; and wherever he found himself mistaken, and those he had appointed proved incapable or unjust, he removed them at once. It was this care of the people that kept him from seeing his princess as often as he would have liked.

Once more Irene heard the bugle blast, and once more she was at the gate to meet her father as he rode up on his great white horse.

After they had been alone for a little while, she asked her question, "Please, King-Papa, will you tell me where I got this pretty ring? Lootie can't remember."

The king looked at it. A strange beautiful smile spread like sunshine over his face, but at the same time a questioning smile spread like moonlight over Irene's.

"It was your queen-mamma's once," he said.

"And why isn't it hers now?" asked Irene.

"She does not need it now," said the king, looking grave.

"Whenever shall I see her?" asked the princess.

"Not for some time yet," answered the king, and tears came into his eyes.

Irene did not remember her mother nor did she know why the tears came into her father's eyes, so she put her arms around his neck and kissed him and asked no more questions.

The king was much disturbed on hearing the report of the gentlemen-at-arms concerning the creatures they had seen. He would have taken Irene away with him that very day, except he knew what the presence of the ring on her finger assured him of. About an hour before he left, Irene saw him go up the old stair, and he did not come down again until they were just ready to start. She thought to herself that he had been up to see the old lady. When he went away this time, he left six more gentlemen so that there might be six of them always on guard.

Now that the spring weather was so lovely, Irene was out on the mountain the greater part of every day. There were lovely primroses in the warmer hollows, and she never tired of them. There were many other flowers all up and down the mountain, and she loved them all. But the primroses were her favorites.

There were goats all about the mountain too, and when the newly-born kids came, she was as pleased with them as with the flowers. The goats mostly belonged to the miners. A few of them belonged to Curdie's mother, but there were a good many wild ones that seemed to belong to nobody. These goats the goblins counted as their own. The cobs set snares and dug pits for them and were not ashamed to take what tame ones happened to be caught.

They did not try, however, to steal them in any other manner, because they were afraid of the dogs that the hill people kept to watch their goats—dogs that would bite their feet.

## 18

# CURDIE'S CLUE

C urdie was as watchful as ever, but was almost getting
tired of his ill success. Every other night he followed
the goblins as they went on digging and boring. He
got as near to them as he could and watched them from behind
stones and rocks, but as yet he seemed no nearer finding out what
they were planning. As always, he kept hold of the end of his
string, while his pickaxe continued to serve as an anchor holding fast the other end just outside the hole by which he entered
the goblins' country. The goblins, hearing no more noise in that
quarter, had ceased to fear an invasion and kept no watch.

One night, after listening until he was nearly asleep with
weariness, he began to roll up his ball and to go home to bed.
It was not long, however, before he began to feel bewildered.
One after another he passed goblin houses—caves, that is—
occupied by goblin families, and he was quite sure there were
many more than he had passed as he came in. He had to use
great caution to pass unseen since they lay so close together.

Could his string have led him wrong? He followed on winding it up as he went, and still it led him into more thickly populated quarters, until he became quite uneasy. He was not afraid of the cobs; he was afraid of not finding his way out. Yet what could he do? He could not wait for the morning, for morning light made no difference here. It was dark, always dark, and if his string failed him he was helpless. He could arrive within one yard of the mine and never know it. But since he could think of nothing better, he determined at least to search for the end of his string and decide, if possible, how it had come to play such a trick on him.

Curdie knew by the growing size of the ball that he was getting pretty near the end of it, when he began to feel a tugging and pulling at it. Then turning a sharp corner, he thought he heard strange sounds. These grew as he went on to a scuffling and growling and squeaking. The noise increased, until he turned a second sharp corner and found himself in the midst of it.

At the same moment he tumbled over a wallowing mass, which he knew must be a knot of the cobs' animals. Before he could recover his feet, they laid great scratches on his face and several severe bites on his legs and arms. But as he scrambled to get up, his hand fell upon his pickaxe, and before the horrid beasts could do him any serious harm, he was swinging it about right and left in the dark. The hideous cries which followed gave Curdie the satisfaction of knowing that he had punished some of them pretty smartly for their rudeness. And by their scampering and their retreating howls, he perceived that he had routed them.

He stood for a little while, weighing his battleaxe in his hand as if it was a most precious lump of metal. But in truth, no lump of gold itself could have been so precious right then as that common tool. Curdie untied the end of the string from it, put the ball in his pocket, and stood, still thinking. It was clear that the cobs' creatures had found his axe, had between them carried it off, and in this way had led him he knew not where. He did not know what he ought to do, until suddenly he became aware of a glimmer of light in the distance. Without a moment's hesitation he set out for it, as fast as the unknown and rugged way would permit. Yet again turning a corner and led by the dim light, he spied something quite new in his experience of the underground regions—a small irregular shape of something shining. Going up to it, he found it was a piece of mica, and the light flickered as if from a fire behind it. After trying in vain for some time to discover where the fire was burning, he came at length to a small chamber in which an opening, high in the wall, revealed a glow beyond. He managed to scramble up to the opening, and then he saw a strange sight.

There sat a small group of goblins around a fire whose smoke vanished into the darkness far aloft. The sides of the cave were full of shining minerals like those of the palace hall, and the company was evidently of a superior order, for every one wore stones about the head, or arms, or waist. Each stone was shining with dull, yet gorgeous colors in the light of the fire. He had not looked long before he recognized the goblin king himself, and Curdie realized that he had made his way into the inner apartment of the royal family. He had never yet had such a good chance of hearing something valuable. He crept through the hole as softly as he could, scrambled a good way down the wall towards them without attracting attention, and then sat down and listened.

The king, evidently the queen, and probably the crown prince and the Prime Minister were talking together. He knew it was the queen by her shoes, for as she warmed her feet at the fire, he saw them quite plainly.

"That will be fun," said the one he took for the crown prince. It was the first whole sentence he heard.

"I don't see why you should think it such a grand affair," said his stepmother, the queen, tossing her head backward.

"You must remember, my spouse," interposed His Majesty, as if making excuse for his son, "he has got the same blood in him. His mother—"

"Don't talk to me of his mother! You positively encourage his unnatural fancies. Whatever belongs to that mother ought to be cut out of him."

"You forget yourself, my dear," said the king.

"I don't," said the queen, "nor you either. If you expect me to approve of such coarse tastes, you will find yourself mistaken. I don't wear shoes for nothing."

"You must acknowledge, however," the king said, with a little groan, "that this is no mere whim of Harelip's, but a matter of state policy. You are well aware that his gratification comes purely from the pleasure of sacrificing himself to the public good. Does it not, Harelip?"

"Yes, Father. Of course it does. Only it would be nice to make her feet like other cobs'. I could have the skin taken off between her toes, and tie them up till they grow together. Then, there will be no occasion for her to wear shoes."

"Do you mean to insinuate I've got toes, you unnatural wretch?" cried the queen, and she moved angrily towards Harelip.

The counselor leaned forward between them as if to address the prince but really to prevent her touching him.

"Your Royal Highness," he said, "possibly requires to be reminded that *you* have got three toes yourself—one on one foot, two on the other."

"Ha! Ha!" shouted the queen triumphantly.

The queen was the only one Curdie could see distinctly. She sat sideways to him, and the light of the fire shone full upon her face. He would not consider her handsome. Her nose was certainly broader at the end than its extreme length; and her eyes, instead of being horizontal, were set up like two perpendicular eggs, one on the broad, the other on the small end; her mouth was no bigger than a small buttonhole until she laughed, when it stretched from ear to ear—only, to be sure, her ears were very nearly in the middle of her cheeks.

Anxious to hear everything they might say, Curdie ventured to slide farther down a smooth part of the rock to a projection below. But whether he was not careful enough or whether the projection gave way, down he came with a rush onto the floor of the cavern, bringing with him a great rumbling shower of stones.

The goblins jumped from their seats more in anger than consternation, for they had not yet seen anything to be afraid of in the palace. But when they saw Curdie with his pick in his hand, their rage became mingled with fear. They took him for the first of an invasion of miners. The king was the handsomest and squarest of all the goblins, and he drew himself up to his full height of four feet and spread himself to his full breadth of three and a half. He strutted up to Curdie, planted himself with outspread feet before him, and said with dignity, "Pray, what right have you in my palace?"

"The right of necessity, Your Majesty," answered Curdie. "I lost my way following the gangs and did not know where I was wandering to."

"How did you get in?"

"By a hole in the mountain."

"But you are a miner! Look at your pickaxe!"

Curdie did look at it, answering, "It is my own axe, Your Majesty, and I came upon it lying on the ground a little way from here. I tumbled over some wild beasts who were playing with it. Look, Your Majesty." And Curdie showed him how he was scratched and bitten.

The king was pleased to find Curdie behave more politely than he had expected based on what his cobs had told him concerning the miners. But he attributed it to the power of his own presence.

"You will oblige me by walking out of my dominions at once," he commanded, well knowing what a mockery lay in the words.

"With pleasure, if Your Majesty will give me a guide," said Curdie.

"I will give you a thousand," said the king with a scoffing air of magnificent liberality.

"One will be quite sufficient," said Curdie.

But the king uttered a strange shout, half halloo, half roar, and in rushed goblins till the cave was swarming. He said something to the first of them which Curdie could not hear, and it was passed from one to another until in a moment the farthest in the crowd had evidently heard and understood it. They began to gather about Curdie in a way he did not relish, and he retreated towards the wall. They pressed upon him.

"Stand back," said Curdie, grasping his pickaxe tighter by his knee.

They only grinned and pressed closer.

Curdie thought quickly and then began to rhyme.

> "Ten, twenty, thirty—
> You're all so very dirty!
> Twenty, thirty, forty—
> You're all so thick and snorty!
>
> "Thirty, forty, fifty—
> You're all so puff-and-snifty!
> Forty, fifty, sixty—
> Beast and man so mixty!
>
> "Fifty, sixty, seventy—
> Mixty, maxty, leaventy!
> Sixty, seventy, eighty—
> All your cheeks so slaty!
>
> "Seventy, eighty, ninety,
> All your hands so flinty!

Eighty, ninety, hundred,

Altogether dundred!"

The goblins fell back a little when he began and made hor-rible grimaces all through the rhyme, as if they were eating something so disagreeable that it set their teeth on edge. But whether it was that the rhyming words were most of them no words at all, since Curdie had made them up on the spur of the moment, or whether it was that the presence of the king and queen gave them courage, but the moment the rhyme was over they crowded in on him again. Out shot a hundred long arms with a multitude of thick nail-less fingers at the ends of them trying to lay hold upon him.

Then Curdie heaved up his axe. But being as gentle as he was courageous and not wishing to kill any of them, he turned the pickaxe over to the end which was square and blunt like a hammer, and with that came down a great blow on the head of the goblin nearest him. Hard as the heads of all goblins were, Curdie thought he must feel that. And so the cob did, no doubt; but he gave only a cry and sprung at Curdie's throat.

Curdie, drew back just in time, and at that critical moment remembered what was the most vulnerable part of the goblin body. He made a sudden rush at the King and stamped with all his might on His Majesty's feet. The king gave a most un-kingly howl and almost fell into the fire. Curdie then rushed into the crowd, stamping right and left. The goblins drew back, howling on every side as he approached. But they were so crowded that few of those he attacked could escape his tread, and the shrieking and roaring that filled the cave would have appalled Curdie but for the good hope it gave him.

They were tumbling over each other in heaps in their eagerness to rush from the cave, when a new assailant suddenly faced him—the Queen. With flaming eyes and flaring nostrils, her hair standing half up from her head, she rushed at him in her shoes made of granite. Curdie would have done almost anything rather than hurt a woman, even if she was a goblin, but this was an affair of life and death. And so forgetting her shoes, he made a great stamp on one of her feet. She instantly returned the stamp causing him frightful pain and almost disabling him. His only real chance with her would have been to attack her granite shoes with his pickaxe, but before he could think of that she had picked him up in her arms and was rushing with him across the cave. She thrust him into a hole in the wall with a force that almost stunned him. But although he could not move, he was not too far injured to hear her great cry and the rush of multitudes of soft feet, followed by the sounds of something heaved up against the rock and then the patter of a multitude of stones falling near him. The shower of stones had not yet ceased when Curdie grew very faint, for his head had been badly cut. At last he lay unconscious.

When he came to himself, there was perfect silence about him and utter darkness—save for one mere glimmer in one tiny spot. He crawled to it and found a heavy slab heaved against the mouth of the hole. One poor little gleam had found its way from the fire past the edge of the rock, but he could not move it a hairbreadth. Against it they had piled a great heap of stones.

Curdie crawled back to where he had been lying in the faint hope of finding his pickaxe, but after a vain search he was at last compelled to acknowledge himself in an evil plight. He sat down and tried to think, but soon fell fast asleep.

# 19

# GOBLIN COUNSELS

Curdie must have slept a long time, for when he awoke he felt wonderfully restored—indeed almost well—and very hungry. There were voices in the outer cave, so he knew that it was night; for the goblins slept during the day and went about their affairs during the night.

In the universal and constant darkness of their dwelling they had no reason to prefer night over day, but because they wanted little to do with the sun people, they chose to be busy then. There was less chance of meeting either the miners below, when they were burrowing, or the people of the mountain above, when they were feeding their sheep or catching their goats. As well, it was when the sun was away that the outside of the mountain was enough like their own dismal regions to be comfortable to their mole eyes. They were quite thoroughly unaccustomed to any light beyond that of their own fires and torches.

Curdie listened, and soon found that they were talking of himself.

"How long will it take?" asked Harelip.

"Not many days, I should think," answered the king. "They are poor feeble creatures, those sun people, and want to be always eating. We can go a week at a time without food, and be all the better for it; but I've been told they eat two or three times every day! Can you believe it? They must be quite hollow inside—not at all like us, nine-tenths of whose bulk is solid flesh and bone. Yes, I judge a week of starvation will do for him."

"If I may be allowed a word," interposed the queen, "and I think I ought to have some voice in the matter—"

"The wretch is entirely at your disposal, my spouse," interrupted the king. "He is your property, since you caught him yourself."

The queen laughed. She seemed in far better humor than the night before.

"I was about to say," she resumed, "that it does seem a pity to waste so much fresh meat."

"What are you thinking of, my love?" said the king. "The very notion of starving him implies that we are not going to give him any meat, either salt or fresh."

"I'm not such a stupid as that comes to," returned Her Majesty. "What I mean is that by the time he is starved there will hardly be a picking upon his bones."

The king gave a great laugh.

"Well, my spouse, you may have him when you like," he said. "I don't fancy him for my part. I am pretty sure he is tough eating."

"That would be to honor him instead of punish his insolence," returned the queen. "But why should our poor creatures be deprived of so much nourishment? Our little dogs and cats and pigs and small bears would enjoy him very much."

"Let it be so by all means," said her husband. "He deserves it. The mischief he might have brought upon us is incalculable."

"For such poor creatures as they are," added the queen, "there is something about those sun people that is very troublesome. I cannot imagine how it is that with such superior strength and skill and understanding as ours, we permit them to exist at all. Why do we not destroy them entirely, and use their cattle and grazing lands at our pleasure? Of course we don't want to live in their horrid country! It is far too glaring for our quieter and more refined tastes. But we might use it as a sort of outpost, you know. We might even keep their great cows and other creatures, and then have a few more luxuries, such as cream and cheese, which at present we only taste occasionally when our brave men succeed in carrying some off from their farms."

"It is worth thinking of," said the king. "And I don't know why you should be the first to suggest it, except that you have a positive genius for conquest. But still, as you say, there is something very troublesome about them. It might be better that we should starve him for a day or two first, so that he may be a little less frisky when we take him out."

"Once there was a goblin
Living in a hole;

Busy he was cobblin'
A shoe without a sole.

"By came a birdie:
'Goblin, what do you do?'
'Cobble at a sturdie
Upper leather shoe.'

" 'What's the good o' that, Sir?'
Said the little bird.
'Why it's very pat, Sir—
Plain without a word.'

" 'Where 'tis all a hole, Sir,
Never can be holes:
Why should their shoes have soles, Sir,
When they've got no souls?' "

"What's that horrible noise?" cried the queen, shuddering
from pot-metal head to granite shoes.

"I declare," said the king with solemn indignation, "it's the
sun creature in the hole!"

"Stop that disgusting noise!" cried the crown prince val-
iantly, getting up and standing in front of the heap of stones
with his face towards Curdie's prison. "Stop it now, or I'll
break your head."

"Break away," shouted Curdie, and began singing again.

"Once there was a goblin,
Living in a hole—"

"I really cannot bear it," said the queen. "If I could only get
at his horrid toes with my slippers again!"

"I think we had better go to bed," said the king.

"It's not time to go to bed," said the queen.

"I would if I was you," called Curdie.

"Impertinent wretch," said the queen with the utmost scorn in her voice.

"An impossible *if,*" said His Majesty with dignity.

"Quite," returned Curdie and began singing again:

> "Go to bed, Goblin, do.
>
> Help the queen take off her shoe.
>
> "If you do, it will disclose
>
> A horrid set of sprouting toes."

"What a lie!" roared the queen in a rage.

"That reminds me," said the king, "that for as long as we have been married, I have never seen your feet, Queen. I think you might take off your shoes when you go to bed. They positively hurt me sometimes."

"I will do as I like," retorted the queen sulkily.

"You ought to do as your own hubby wishes you," said the king.

"I will not," said the queen.

"Then I insist upon it," said the king.

Apparently His Majesty approached the queen for the purpose of following the advice sung by Curdie, for the latter heard a scuffle, and then a great roar from the king.

"Will you be quiet now?" said the queen wickedly.

"Yes, yes, Queen. I only meant to coax you."

"I'm going to bed," cried the queen triumphantly. "And as long as I am queen, I will sleep in my shoes. It is my royal privilege. Harelip, go to bed."

"I'm going," said Harelip sleepily.

"So am I," said the king.

"Come along then," said the queen.

Curdie heard only a muttered reply in the distance, and then the cave was quite still.

They had left the fire burning, and the light came through brighter than before. Curdie thought it was time to try again to see if anything could be done. But he found he could not get even a finger through the chink between the slab and the rock. He gave a great rush against the slab with his shoulder, but it yielded no more than if it had been part of the rock. All he could do was to sit down and think again.

By and by he determined that he would pretend to be dying, in the hope they might take him out before his strength was too much exhausted to let him have a chance. Then if he could but find his axe again, he would have no fear of them; and if it were not for the queen's horrid shoes, he would have no fear at all.

Meantime, until they would come back again at night, there was nothing for him to do but forge new rhymes which were now his only weapons. He had no intention of using them yet, but it was well to have a stock, for he might live to need them, and the manufacture of them would help to while away the time.

## 20

# IRENE'S CLUE

E arly that same morning, the princess woke in a terrible fright. There was a hideous noise in her room— creatures snarling and hissing and rocketing about as if they were fighting. The moment she came to herself, she remembered something she had not thought of again until now—what her grandmother told her to do when she was frightened. She immediately took off her ring and put it under her pillow. As she did so she imagined that she felt a finger and thumb take it gently from her hand.

*It must be my grandmother!* she said to herself, and the thought gave her such courage that she stopped to put on her dainty little slippers before running from the room. While she was putting on her shoes, she caught sight of a long sky-blue cloak thrown over the back of a chair by the bedside. She had never seen it before, but it was evidently waiting for her. She put it on, and then began feeling with the forefinger of her right hand. She soon found her grandmother's thread, and she proceeded to follow it at once, expecting it would lead her straight up the old stair. When she reached the door, she found that the thread went down and ran along the floor, so that she had almost to crawl in order to keep a hold of it.

Then, to her surprise—and somewhat to her dismay—she found that instead of leading her up towards the stair, it turned down in quite the opposite direction. It led her through narrow passages towards the kitchen, turning aside before her and guiding her instead to a door which connected with a small back yard. Some of the maids were already up, and so this door was standing open. Across the yard the thread still ran along the ground until it brought her to a door in the garden wall which opened onto the mountainside. When Irene had passed through, the thread rose to about half her height, and she could hold it with ease as she walked. It led her straight up the mountain.

The cause of her alarm was less frightful than she had first supposed. The cook's great black cat, pursued by the housekeeper's terrier, had bounced against her bedroom door. The door had not been properly fastened, and the two animals had burst into her room together and commenced a battle royal. How Nurse was able to sleep through it was a mystery.

It was a clear warm morning. The wind blew deliciously over the mountainside. Here and there Irene saw a late primrose, but she did not stop to look. The sky was mottled with small clouds. The dew lay in round drops upon the leaves, and hung like tiny diamond earrings from the blades of grass about her path.

*How lovely that bit of gossamer is!* thought the princess, looking at a long undulating line that shone at some distance from her up the hill. She soon discovered that it was her own thread that she saw shining before her in the light of the morning leading her she knew not where. She had never in her life been out before sunrise, and everything was so fresh and cool and lively and full of something coming, that she felt too happy to be afraid of anything.

After leading her up a good distance, the thread turned to the left and down the path upon which she and Lootie had met Curdie. But she didn't think of that now, for in the morning light with its far outlook over the country, no path could have been more open and airy and cheerful. She could see the road almost to the horizon along which she had so often watched her king-papa and his troop come shining with the bugle-blast cleaving the air before them. It was a familiar road to her.

Down and down the path went, then up and then down and then up again, getting more rugged as it went. Yet still along the path went the silvery thread, and still along the thread went Irene's rosy-tipped forefinger. By and by she came to a little stream that prattled down the hill, and up beside the stream went both path and thread. The path grew still rougher and steeper, and the mountain grew wilder, till Irene began to think she was going a very long way from home. When she turned to look back, she saw that the level country had vanished and the rough bare mountain had closed in about her.

But still on went the thread, and on went the princess. Everything around her was getting brighter and brighter until at length the sun's first rays alighted on the top of a rock before her. Then she saw that the little stream ran out of a hole in that rock, and that the path did not go past the rock. A shudder ran through her from head to foot when she found that the thread was actually taking her into the hole out of which the stream ran. The water ran *out* babbling joyously, but she had to go *in*.

She did not hesitate but walked right into the hole. It was high enough to let her walk in without stooping. For a way there was a little glimmer of light, but at the first turn it all but ceased, and before she had gone many paces she was in total darkness. And then she began to be frightened indeed.

She kept feeling the thread backwards and forwards, and as she went farther and farther into the darkness of the great hollow mountain, she kept thinking more and more about her grandmother. She thought of all that her grandmother had said to her, how kind she had been, and how beautiful she was. She remembered all about her lovely room, and the fire of roses, and the great lamp that sent its light through stone walls. And she became more and more certain that the thread could not have come here by itself, and that her grandmother must have sent it.

But it tried her dreadfully when the path went down very steep, and especially when she came to places where she had to go down rough stairs, and even sometimes a ladder. Through one narrow passage after another, over lumps of rock and sand and clay, the thread guided her, until she came to a small hole through which she had to creep. Finding no change on the other side, she thought, *Shall I ever find my way back?* She was surprised at herself that she was not ten times more frightened, and felt as if she were only walking in the story of a dream. Sometimes she heard the dull noise of water gurgling inside the rock. By and by she heard the sounds of blows, which came nearer then again grew duller and almost died away. She turned in a hundred directions, obedient to the guiding thread.

At last she spied a dull red glow and came up to the mica window, and from there away and around right into a cavern where the red embers of a fire glowed. Here the thread began to rise again as high as her head and higher still. She feared she would lose her hold and feared too that pulling it down might break the thread.

Presently she came to a huge heap of stones, piled in a slope against the wall of the cavern. She climbed up on these, and soon recovered the level of the thread, only to find the very next moment that the thread itself vanished through the heap of stones. She was standing on top of the heap with her face to the solid rock. For one terrible moment she felt as if her grandmother had forsaken her. The thread which the spiders had spun far over the seas, which her grandmother had sat in the moonlight and spun again for her, which she had tempered in the rose fire and tied to her opal ring, this thread had left her and had gone where she could no longer follow. It had brought her into a horrible cavern, and left her there! She was forsaken indeed.

*When shall I wake?* she said to herself in an agony, yet she knew at the same moment that it was no dream.

It was well that she did not know what creatures, one of them with stone shoes on her feet, were lying in the very next cave. But neither did she know who was on the other side of the slab.

At last the thought struck her that perhaps she could follow the thread backwards out of the mountain and home. She rose at once and found the thread. But the instant she tried to feel it backwards, it vanished from her touch. Forwards, it led her hand up to the heap of stones—backwards, it seemed nowhere.

And without the light of the fire, she could not see the thread either.

# 21

# The Escape

T he princess kept touching the thread, following it with her finger right up to the stones into which it disappeared. By and by she began to poke her finger into the hole between the stones as far as she could. All at once it came to her that she might be able to remove some of the stones and see where the thread went next. Almost laughing at herself for not thinking of this sooner, she jumped to her feet, her fear vanished.

Once more she was certain her grandmother's thread could not have brought her there just to leave her there. She began to throw away the stones from the top as fast as she could, sometimes taking two or three in a handful, sometimes using both hands to lift one. After clearing them away a little, she found that the thread turned straight downwards. Since the heap sloped a good deal, growing wider towards its base, she had to throw away a multitude of stones in order to follow the thread. Soon it turned first sideways in one direction, then sideways in another, and then shot, at various angles, hither and thither inside the heap, so that Irene was afraid that to clear the thread she would have to remove the whole huge heap of stones.

She was dismayed at the very idea, but set to work with a will. Her back began to ache, and her fingers and hands began to bleed, but she worked on, sustained by the pleasure of seeing the heap slowly diminish and begin to show itself restacked on the opposite side of the fire. As often as she uncovered a turn of the thread, instead of lying loose upon the stone, it tightened up. This made her quite sure that her grandmother was at the end of it somewhere, and she took courage.

She had got about halfway down when she was startled by a voice that broke out singing quite near to her ears.

> "Jabber, bother, smash!
> You'll have it all in a crash.
> Jabber, smash, bother!
> You'll have the worst of the pother.
> Smash, bother, jabber!—"

Here Curdie stopped, either because he could not find a rhyme to "jabber," or because he remembered what he had forgotten, that his plan was to make the goblins think he was getting weak. But he had uttered enough to let Irene know who he was.

"It's Curdie!" she cried joyfully.

"Hush, hush!" came Curdie's voice again from somewhere. "Speak softly."

"Why? *You* were singing loud!" said Irene.

"Yes. But they know I am here. They don't know that you are. Who are you?"

"I'm Irene," answered the princess. "I know who you are quite well. You're Curdie."

"How ever did you come here, Irene?"

"My great-great-grandmother sent me, and I think I know why. You can't get out, I think."

"No, I can't. What are you doing?"

"Clearing away a huge heap of stones."

"There's a princess," exclaimed Curdie, in a tone of delight, but still speaking in little more than a whisper. "I can't think how you got here though."

"My grandmother led me with her thread."

"I don't know what you mean," said Curdie, "but you're there, so it doesn't much matter."

"Yes, it does," returned Irene. "I should never have been here unless she led me."

"You can tell me all about it when we get out, but there's no time to lose now," said Curdie.

And Irene went back to work, as fresh as when she began.

"There's such a lot of stones!" she said. "It will take me a long time to get them all pulled away."

"How far on have you got?" asked Curdie.

"I've got about half cleared away, but the other half is so much bigger."

"I don't think you will have to move all of the lower half. Do you find a great slab leaned up against the wall?"

Irene looked and felt about with her hands. Soon she perceived the outlines of the slab.

"Yes," she answered, "I do."

"Then I think," responded Curdie, "when you have cleared the slab about halfway down, or a bit more, I may be able to push it over."

"I must follow my thread," returned Irene, "whatever I do."

"What do you mean?" exclaimed Curdie.

"You will see when you get out," answered the princess, and went on working harder than ever.

She was soon satisfied that what Curdie wanted her to do and what the thread wanted her to do were one and the same thing. She saw that by following the turns of the thread, she had been clearing the face of the slab. A little more than halfway down, the thread went through the chink between the slab and the wall right into the place where Curdie was confined. She could not follow it any farther until the slab was pushed out of her way.

As soon as she found this out, she called to him in a joyous whisper, "Now, Curdie, I think if you were to give a great push, the slab would tumble over."

"Stand clear of it then," said Curdie, "and let me know when you are ready."

Irene got off the heap and stood to one side of it. "Now, Curdie!"

Curdie gave a great rush with his shoulder against it. Over tumbled the slab onto the heap, and out of the hole crept Curdie.

"You've saved my life, Irene!" he whispered.

"I'm so glad, Curdie. Let's get out of this horrid place as fast as we can."

"That's easier said than done," returned he.

"Oh, no, it's quite easy," said Irene. "We have only to follow my thread. I am sure that it's going to take us out now."

She had already begun to follow it over the fallen slab into the hole, while Curdie was searching the floor of the cavern for his pickaxe.

"Here it is!" he cried. "No, it is not," he added, in a disappointed tone. "But what is this then? I declare it's a torch. That is jolly! It's better almost than my pickaxe." And he lighted the torch by blowing the last embers of the expiring fire.

The lighted torch cast a glare into the great darkness of the huge cavern, and Curdie caught sight of Irene disappearing through the hole out of which he had himself just come.

"Where are you going there?" he cried. "That's where I couldn't get out."

"But this is the way my thread goes," whispered Irene, "and I must follow it."

*What nonsense the child talks!* Curdie thought to himself. *I must follow her, and see that she comes to no harm. She will soon find she can't get out that way, and then she will come with me.*

So he crept over the slab once more into the hole with his torch in his hand. But when he looked around, he could see her nowhere. He discovered that although the hole was narrow, it was much longer than he had supposed. In one direction the roof came down very low, and the hole went off in a narrow passage. He could not see the end, but the princess must have crept in there. He got on his knees and one hand, holding the torch with the other, and crept after her. The hole twisted about, in some parts so low that he could hardly get through, in others so high that he could not see the roof. But everywhere it was narrow—far too narrow for a goblin to get through.

Curdie was beginning to feel that something must have befallen the princess, when he heard her voice very close to his ear, whispering, "Aren't you coming, Curdie?"

And when he turned the next corner there she stood waiting for him.

"I knew you couldn't go wrong in that narrow hole, but now you must keep by me, for here is a great wide place," she said.

"I can't understand it," said Curdie, half to himself, half to Irene.

"Never mind," she returned. "Wait until we get out."

Curdie was utterly astonished that she had already gotten so far, and by a path he had known nothing of. He thought it was better to let her do as she pleased.

*At all events*, he thought again to himself, *miner as I am, I do not know this way that she seems to know something about. How she should know passes my comprehension. But it is just as likely for her to find her way as I am to find mine, so I will follow. We can't be much worse off than we are now anyhow.*

Reasoning thus, he followed her a few steps and came out in another great cavern. Irene walked across it in a straight line, as confidently as if she knew every step of the way. Curdie followed, flashing his torch about and trying to see something of what lay around them. Suddenly his light fell upon something that Irene was passing by. It was a platform of rock raised a few feet from the floor and covered with sheepskins. On the platform lay two sleeping figures which Curdie recognized at once as the king and queen of the goblins. He lowered his torch instantly lest the light should awaken them, and as he did, it flashed upon his pickaxe lying by the side of the queen. Her hand lay close to the handle of it.

"Stop one moment," he whispered. "Hold my torch, and don't let the light on their faces."

Irene shuddered when she saw the frightful creatures whom she had already passed without seeing, but she did as Curdie requested. She turned her back and held the torch low in front of her. Curdie drew his pickaxe carefully away. Then he spied one of the queen's feet projecting out from under the skins. The great clumsy granite shoe was a temptation not to be resisted. He took hold of it and cautiously drew it off. He saw to his astonishment that what he had sung in ignorance to annoy the queen, was actually true. She *did* have six horrible toes. Overjoyed at his success, and seeing by the huge bump in the sheepskins where the other foot was, he proceeded to lift the covers gently. If he could succeed in carrying away the other shoe as well, he would be no more afraid of the goblins than of so many flies. But as he pulled at the second shoe, the queen gave a growl and sat up in bed. The same instant the king awoke also and sat up beside her.

"Run, Irene!" cried Curdie. Though he was not in the least bit afraid for himself, he did fear for the princess.

Irene looked once around, saw the fearful creatures awake, and like the wise princess she was, dashed the torch on the ground. The flame went out, and she called to him, "Here, Curdie, take my hand."

He darted to her side, forgetting neither the queen's shoe nor his pickaxe, and caught hold of her hand. She sped fearlessly on where her thread guided her. They heard the queen give a great bellow, but they had a good start, especially since it would take some time before the king could get torches lighted to pursue them. Just as they thought they saw a gleam behind them, the thread brought them to a very narrow opening, through which Irene crept easily, and Curdie with difficulty.

"Now," said Curdie, "I think we shall be safe."

"Of course we shall," returned Irene.

"Why do you think so?" asked Curdie.

"Because my grandmother is taking care of us."

"That's all nonsense," said Curdie. "I don't know what you mean."

"Then if you don't know what I mean, what right have you to call it nonsense?" asked the princess, a bit offended.

"I beg your pardon, Irene," said Curdie.

"Of course," returned the princess. "But why do you think we will be safe?"

"Because the king and queen are far too stout to get through that hole."

"There might be ways around," said the princess.

"To be sure, there might. We are not out of here yet," acknowledged Curdie.

"But what do you mean by the king and queen?" asked the princess. "I would never call such creatures as those a king and a queen."

"Their own people do though," answered Curdie.

The princess asked more questions, and Curdie gave her a full account as they walked leisurely along. He told her not only of the character and habits of the goblins as he knew them, but also of his own adventures with them, beginning from the very night in which he had met her and Lootie upon the mountain. When he had finished, he begged Irene to tell him how it was that she had come to his rescue.

Irene had a long story to tell too, which she did in rather a roundabout manner. Curdie interrupted her with many questions about things she had not explained. But since he did not believe more than half of her tale, everything was as unaccountable to him as before. He was perplexed as to what he must think of the princess. He did not believe that she was deliberately telling stories, so the only conclusion he could come to was that Lootie had been playing tricks on the princess, inventing no end of lies to frighten her for some unknown reason.

"But how was it that Lootie allowed you to go into the mountains alone?" he asked.

"Nurse knows nothing about it. I left her fast asleep—at least I think so."

"But," persisted Curdie, "how did you find your way to me?"

"I told you already," answered Irene, "by keeping my finger upon my grandmother's thread, just as I am doing now."

"You don't mean you've got the thread there?"

"Of course I do. I have told you so ten times already. I have hardly—except when I was removing the stones—taken my finger off it. There!" she added, guiding Curdie's hand to the thread, "you feel it yourself, don't you?"

"I feel nothing at all," replied Curdie.

"Then what is the matter with your finger? I feel it perfectly. To be sure it is very thin, and in the sunlight looks just like the thread of a spider, but I don't know why you shouldn't feel it as well as I do."

Curdie was too polite to say he did not believe there was any thread there at all. What he did say was, "Well, I cannot feel it."

"I can, and you had better be glad of that, for it will do for both of us."

"We're not out yet," said Curdie.

"We soon shall be," returned Irene confidently. And now the thread went downwards, and led Irene's hand to a hole in the floor of the cavern where they could hear the sound of running water.

"It goes into the ground now, Curdie," she said, stopping.

He had been listening to another sound, which his practiced ear had caught long ago. It had been growing louder. It was the noise the goblin-miners made at their work, and they seemed to be very close now. Irene heard it the moment she stopped.

"What is that noise?" she asked. "Do you know, Curdie?"

"Yes. It is the goblins digging and burrowing," he answered.

"And you don't know what they do it for?"

"No, I haven't the least idea. Would you like to see them?" he asked, wishing to try once more to learn their secret.

"If my thread took me there, I wouldn't much mind. But I don't want to see them, and I can't leave my thread. It leads me down into the hole, and we had better go at once."

"Very well. Shall I go in first?" said Curdie.

"No. You can't feel the thread," she answered, stepping down through a narrow break in the floor of the cavern. "Oh!" she cried, "I am in the water. It is running strong—but it is not deep, and there is just room to walk. Make haste, Curdie."

He tried, but the hole was too small for him to get in.

"Go on a little bit," he said, shouldering his pickaxe. In a few moments he had cleared a larger opening and followed her. They went on, down and down with the running water. Curdie feared that the thread was leading them to some terrible place in the heart of the mountain. And in one or two places he had to break away the rock to make room before even Irene could get through—at least without hurting herself.

Finally they spied a glimmer of light, and in a minute more they were almost blinded by the bright sunlight into which they emerged. It took a little while before the princess could see well enough to realize that they stood in her own garden right by the seat where she and her king-papa had sat that afternoon. She danced and clapped her hands with delight.

"Now, Curdie!" she cried, "don't you believe now what I told you about my grandmother and her thread?"

For she had known all along that Curdie did not believe what she told him.

"There! Don't you see it shining on before us?" she added.

"I don't see anything," persisted Curdie.

"Then you must believe without seeing," said the princess; "for you can't deny that it has brought us safely out of the mountain."

"I can't deny that we are out of the mountain. And I should be very ungrateful indeed to deny that it was you who had brought me out."

"I couldn't have done it without the thread," persisted Irene.

"That's the part I don't understand."

"Oh, well, come along. Nurse will get you something to eat, and I am sure you must want that very much."

"Indeed I do. But my father and mother will be anxious about me. I must make haste—first up the mountain to tell my mother, and then down into the mine again to let my father know."

"Very well, Curdie. But you can't get out of the garden without coming this way, so I will take you through the house, for that is nearest."

They met no one along the way, for just as before, the people were here and there and everywhere searching for the missing princess. When Irene and Curdie entered the house, the thread went up the old staircase and a new thought struck her.

She turned to Curdie and said, "My grandmother wants me. Please come up with me and see her. Then you will know that I have been telling you the truth. Do come—to please me, Curdie. I can't bear for you to think that what I say is not true."

"I never doubted that you yourself believed what you said," returned Curdie. "I only thought that you had some fancy in your head that was not correct."

"But do come."

Though the little miner felt shy in what seemed to him a huge grand house, he yielded, and followed her up the stair.

## 22

# THE OLD LADY
# AND CURDIE

Up the stair they went then, and the next and the next, and through the long rows of empty rooms, and up the little tower stair. Irene was growing happier and happier as she ascended. But there was no answer when she knocked at the door of the workroom, nor could she hear any sound of the spinning wheel. Once more her heart sank within her. Then she turned and knocked at the other door.

"Come in," answered the sweet voice of her grandmother. Irene opened the door and entered, followed by Curdie.

"I've been waiting for you," said the lady, who was seated by a fire of red roses mingled with white, "and indeed getting a little anxious about you. I was beginning to think that I had better go and fetch you myself."

As she spoke she took the princess in her arms and placed her upon her lap. She was dressed in white now and looked more lovely than ever.

"I've brought Curdie, Grandmother. He wouldn't believe what I told him, and so I've brought him."

"Yes—I see him. He is a good boy, Curdie, and a brave boy. Aren't you glad you've got him out?"

"Yes, Grandmother. But it wasn't very good of him not to believe me when I was telling him the truth."

"People must believe what they can. Those who believe more must not be hard upon those who believe less. I doubt if you would have believed it all yourself, if you hadn't seen some of it."

"I dare say you are right, Grandmother. But surely he'll believe now."

"I don't know that," replied her grandmother.

"Won't you, Curdie?" said Irene, looking round at him as she asked the question. He was standing in the middle of the floor, staring, and looking strangely bewildered. She thought this came of his astonishment at the beauty of the lady. "Make a bow to my grandmother, Curdie," she said.

"I don't see any grandmother," answered Curdie rather gruffly.

"You don't see my grandmother, when I'm sitting in her lap?"

"No, I don't," answered Curdie, in an offended tone.

"Don't you see the lovely fire of roses—white ones amongst them this time?" asked Irene, almost as bewildered as he.

"No, I don't."

"Nor the blue bed? Nor the rose-colored counterpane? Nor the beautiful light, like the moon, hanging from the roof?"

"You're making fun of me, Your Royal Highness, and after what we have come through together this day, I don't think it is kind of you," said Curdie, feeling very much hurt.

"Then what *do* you see?" asked Irene. She realized that for her not to believe him was at least as bad as for him not to believe her.

"I see a big, bare, garret room—like the one in my mother's cottage, only big enough to hold the cottage itself and leave a good margin all round," answered Curdie.

"And what more do you see?"

"I see a tub, and a heap of musty straw, and a withered apple, and a ray of sunlight coming through a hole in the middle of the roof and shining on your head, and making all the place look a curious dusky brown. I think you had better go down to the nursery like a good girl."

"But don't you hear my grandmother talking to me?" asked Irene, almost crying.

"No. I hear the cooing of a lot of pigeons. If you won't come down, I will go without you. That might be better anyhow, for I'm sure nobody who met us would believe a word we said to them. They would think we made it all up. I don't expect anybody but my own father and mother to believe me. They know I wouldn't tell a story."

"And yet you won't believe me, Curdie?" The princess was now fairly crying with vexation and sorrow at the gulf between her and Curdie.

"No. I can't, and I can't help it," said Curdie, turning to leave the room.

"What shall I do, Grandmother?" cried the princess.

"You must give him time," said her grandmother, "and you must be content not to be believed for a while. It is very hard to bear; but I have had to bear it, and shall have to bear it many a time yet. I will take care of what Curdie thinks of you in the end. You must let him go now."

"You're not coming, are you?" asked Curdie.

"No, Curdie. My grandmother says I must let you go. Turn to the right when you get to the bottom of all the stairs, and that will take you to the hall where the great door is."

"Oh, don't doubt that I can find my way—without you, princess, or your old grannie's thread either," said Curdie quite rudely.

"Curdie!"

"I wish I had gone home at once. I'm very much obliged to you, Irene, for getting me out of that hole, but I wish you hadn't made a fool of me afterwards."

He said this as he opened the door and without another word, he went down the stair. Irene listened with dismay to his departing footsteps.

Then turning again to the lady, she asked, "What does it all mean, Grandmother?"

"It means, my love, that I did not mean to show myself. Curdie is not yet able to believe some things. Seeing is not believing; it is only seeing. You remember I told you that if Lootie were to see me, she would rub her eyes, forget the half she saw and call the other half nonsense."

"Yes, but I should have thought Curdie—"

"You are right. Curdie is much farther on than Lootie, and you will see what will come of it. But in the meantime you must be content to be misunderstood for a while. We are all very anxious to be understood, and it is very hard not to be. But there is one thing much more necessary."

"What is that, Grandmother?"

"To understand other people."

"Yes, Grandmother. I must be fair. If I'm not fair to other people, I'm not worth being understood myself. Yes, I see. Since Curdie can't help it, I will not be vexed with him. I will wait."

"There's my own dear child," said her grandmother, and held her close.

"Why weren't you spinning when we came up, Grandmother?" asked Irene, after a few moments' silence.

"I've nobody to spin for just now. I never spin without knowing for whom I am spinning."

"There is one thing that puzzles me," said the princess. "How will you get the thread back out of the mountain again? Surely you won't have to make another for me? That would be such trouble!"

The lady set her down and went to the fire. She put in her hand, and then drew it out again. She held up the shining ball between her finger and thumb.

"I've got it now, you see," she said, coming back to the princess. "It is all ready for you when you need it."

Going to her cabinet, she put it in the same drawer as before.

"And here is your ring," she added, taking it from the little finger of her left hand and putting it on the forefinger of Irene's right hand.

"Thank you, Grandmother! I feel so safe now!"

"You are very tired, my child," the lady went on. "Your hands are hurt with the stones, and I have counted nine bruises on you. Just look at yourself."

And she held up a little mirror which she had brought from the cabinet. The princess burst into a merry laugh at the sight. She was so bedraggled from the stream and dirty from creeping through narrow places, that if she had seen this reflection without knowing it was a reflection, she would have taken herself for some gypsy child whose face was washed and hair combed only once in a month. The lady laughed too, and lifting her again carried her to the side of the room. Irene wondered but asked no questions. The lady lay her in the large silver bath.

"Do not be afraid, my child."

"No, Grandmother," answered the princess, and the next instant she sank into the clear cool water.

When she opened her eyes, she saw nothing but a strange lovely blue over and beneath and all about her. The lady and the beautiful room had vanished from her sight, and she seemed utterly alone. But she was not afraid; she felt perfectly blissful. From somewhere came the voice of the lady, singing a strange sweet song, of which she could distinguish every word, but not with understanding. Nor could she remember a single line after it was gone. It vanished like a dream as fast as it came.

How long she lay in the water Irene did not know. It seemed a pleasantly long time. But at last she felt the grandmother's beautiful hands lay hold of her, and through the gurgling water she was lifted out into the lovely room. The lady carried her to the fire, and dried her tenderly with the softest towel. It was so different from Lootie's drying. When the lady was done, she stooped to the fire and drew from it Irene's nightgown, as white as snow.

"How delicious!" exclaimed the princess. "It smells of all the roses in the world, I think."

When she stood up on the floor, she felt as if she had been made over again. Every bruise and all weariness were gone, and her hands were soft and whole as ever.

"Now I am going to put you to bed for a good sleep," said her grandmother.

"But what will Lootie think? And what am I to say to her when she asks me where I have been?"

"Don't trouble yourself about it. It will all come right." And her grandmother laid her into the blue bed under the rosy counterpane.

"There is just one thing more," said Irene. "I am a little worried about Curdie. Since I brought him into the house, I ought to have seen him safely on his way home."

"I took care of Curdie," answered the lady. "I told you to let him go, and therefore I was bound to look after him. Nobody saw him, and he is now eating a good dinner in his mother's cottage far up in the mountain."

"Then I will go to sleep," said Irene, and in just a few minutes she was.

# 23

# CURDIE AND HIS MOTHER

Curdie went up the mountain neither whistling nor singing, for he was vexed with Irene for *taking him in*, as he called it. He was vexed with himself as well for having spoken to her so angrily.

His mother gave a cry of joy when she saw him and set about at once getting him something to eat. She asked him questions, which he answered, but not so cheerfully as usual. When his meal was ready, she left him to eat it and hurried to the mine to let his father know he was safe. When she came back, she found him fast asleep upon her bed, and he slept soundly until his father came home in the evening.

"Now, Curdie," his mother said, as they sat at supper, "tell us the whole story from beginning to end, just as it happened."

Curdie obeyed and told everything up to the point where they came out upon the lawn in the garden of the king's house.

"And what happened after that?" asked his mother. "You haven't told us that part. You ought to be very happy at having got away from those goblins, but I have never seen you so gloomy. There must be something more. Nor do you speak of that lovely child as I should like to hear you. She saved your life at the risk of her own, and yet somehow you don't seem to think much of it."

"She talked such nonsense," answered Curdie, "and told me a pack of things that weren't a bit true."

"What were they?" asked his father. "Your mother may be able to throw some light upon them."

Then Curdie made a clean breast of it and told them everything.

They all sat silent for some time, pondering the strange tale. At last Curdie's mother spoke.

"You confess, my boy," she said, "that there is something about the whole affair you do not understand?"

"Yes, of course, Mother," he answered. "I cannot understand how a girl knowing nothing about the mountain, or even that I was shut up in it, should come all that way alone straight to where I was. Nor do I understand how after getting me out of the hole, she led me straight out of the mountain too, where I would not have known one step of the way even if it had been as light as day."

"Then you have no right to say what she told you was not true. She did lead you out, and she must have had something to guide her. Why not a thread as well as a rope, or anything else? There is something you cannot explain, and her explanation may be the right one."

"It's no explanation at all, Mother. I can't believe it."

"That may be only because you do not understand it. If you did, you might find it is a good explanation, and believe it thoroughly. I don't blame you for not being able to believe it, but I do blame you for fancying that such a child would try to deceive you. Why should she? Depend upon it, Curdie, she told you all she knew, and until you find a better way of accounting for it all, you might at least be more sparing of your judgment."

"That is what something inside me has been saying all the time," said Curdie, hanging down his head. "But what do you make of the grandmother? That is what I can't get over. To take me up to an old garret and try to persuade me against the sight of my own eyes that it was a beautiful room with blue walls and silver stars and no end of things in it, when there was nothing there but an old tub and a withered apple and a heap of straw and a sunbeam! She might have had some old woman there at least to pass for her precious grandmother."

"Did she speak as if she saw those other things herself, Curdie?"

"Yes. That's what bothers me. You would have thought she really believed that she saw every one of the things she talked about. And not one of them there! It was too mean, I say."

"Perhaps some people can see things other people can't see, Curdie," said his mother very gravely. "I would like to tell you something I saw myself once—only I fear that you won't believe me either."

"Oh, Mother!" cried Curdie, "I don't deserve that surely."

"But what I am going to tell you is very strange," persisted his mother; "and you may say that I must have been dreaming, and I know that I was not asleep."

"Do tell me, Mother. Perhaps it will help me to think better of the princess."

"That is why I am tempted to tell you," replied his mother. "But first, I may as well mention that, according to old whispers, there is something very unusual about the king's family, and the queen was of the same blood, for they were cousins of some degree. There were strange stories told concerning them—all good stories—but strange, very strange. I only remember the faces of my grandmother and my mother as they whispered together about them. They never spoke aloud. There was wonder and awe in their eyes, but no fear."

"But this is what I saw myself: Your father was going to work in the mine one night, and I had been down with his supper. It was not very long before you were born. He came with me to the mouth of the mine, but let me walk home alone since I knew the way almost as well as the floor of our own cottage. It was pretty dark, but I got along perfectly well, never thinking of being afraid, until I reached a spot you know well enough, Curdie. It was the spot where the path has to make a sharp turn out of the way of a great rock on the left-hand side. When I got there, I was suddenly surrounded by about half a dozen of the cobs. Although I had heard tell of them often enough, they were the first I had ever seen. One of them blocked the path, and they all began tormenting and teasing me in a way that makes me shudder to think of even now."

"If I had only been with you!" cried father and son in a breath.

The mother gave a funny little smile and went on.

"They had some of their horrible creatures with them too, and I must confess I was dreadfully frightened. They tore at my clothes, and I was afraid they were going to tear me to pieces as well, when suddenly a great white soft light shone upon me. I looked up. A broad ray, like a shining road, came down from a large globe of silvery light not very high up. It was not quite so high as the horizon, so it could not have been a new star or another moon or anything of that sort. The cobs dropped tormenting me and looked dazed. I thought they were going to run away, but presently they started in again. The same moment, however, down the path from the globe of light came a bird, shining like silver in the sun. It gave a few rapid flaps first, and then with its wings straight out, shot, sliding down the slope of the light. It looked to me just like a white pigeon. But whatever it was, when the cobs caught sight of it coming straight down upon them, they took to their heels and scampered away, leaving me safe, only much frightened. As soon as it had sent them off, the bird went gliding again up the light, and the moment it reached the globe the light disappeared. It was just as if a shutter had been closed over a window, and I saw it no more. But I had no more trouble with the cobs that night or ever after."

"How strange," said Curdie.

"Yes, it was strange; but I can't help believing that it happened, whether you do or not," said his mother.

"That is exactly what your mother told me the very next morning," said his father.

"You don't think I'm doubting my own mother?" cried Curdie.

"There are other people in the world just as worth believing as your own mother," said his mother. "There are mothers far more likely to tell lies than the little girl I saw talking to the primroses a few weeks ago, Mr. Curdie. If she were to lie, I should begin to doubt my own word."

"But princesses have told lies as well as other people," said Curdie.

"Yes, but not princesses like that child. She's a good girl, I am certain, and that's worth more than being a princess. Depend upon it. You will be sorry for behaving so to her, Curdie. You ought at least to have held your tongue."

"I am sorry now," answered Curdie.

"You ought to go and tell her so then."

"I don't see how I could manage that. They won't let a miner boy like me have a word with her alone, and I can't tell her in front of that nurse of hers. She'd be asking ever so many questions, and I don't know how many the little princess would like me to answer. She told me that Lootie didn't know anything about her coming to get me out of the mountain, and I am certain Lootie would have stopped her had she known. But I may have a chance to speak with her sometime, and meantime I must try to do something for her. I think, Father, I have got on the goblins' track at last."

"Have you, indeed, my boy?" said Peter. "You have worked very hard for some news. What have you found out?"

"It's difficult, you know, Father, inside the mountain in the dark not knowing what turns you have taken to tell the lie of things outside."

"Impossible, my boy, without a chart or at least a compass," returned his father.

"Well, I think I have nearly discovered in what direction the cobs are mining. If I am right, I know something else. And taken together one and one will lead to three."

"They very often do, Curdie, as we miners ought to be very well aware. Now tell us, my boy, what the two things are, and see whether we can guess at the same third as you."

"I don't see what that has to do with the princess," interposed his mother.

"I will soon let you see that, Mother. You may think me foolish, but until I am sure, I am more determined than ever to go on with my observations. As we came to the channel through which we got out, I heard the miners at work somewhere near—I think down below us. Ever since I began watching them, they have mined a good half mile in a straight line. As far as I can tell, they are working in no other part of the mountain. I think they are working towards the king's house, and what I want to do tonight is to make sure whether they are or not. I will take a light with me—"

"Oh, Curdie," cried his mother, "then they will see you."

"I'm no more afraid of them now than I was before," rejoined Curdie, "now that I've got this precious shoe. They can't make another in a hurry, and one bare foot will do for my purposes. Even though she is a woman, I won't spare her next time. But I will be careful with my light."

"Go on then, and tell us what you mean to do."

"I mean to take a bit of paper with me and a pencil, and go in at the mouth of the stream by which we came out. I shall mark on the paper as near as I can the angle of every turning I take until I find the cobs at work. I will get a good idea in what direction they are going, and if it should prove to be nearly parallel with the stream, I will know it is towards the king's house they are working."

"And what if that is so? How much wiser will you be then?"

"Wait a minute, Mother dear. I told you that when I came upon the royal family in the cave, they were talking of their prince Harelip marrying a sun woman—that means one of us—one with toes to her feet. Now in one of the speeches they made at their great gathering that night, a goblin said that peace would be secured for a generation at least by the pledge the prince 'would hold for the good behavior of her relatives.' That's what he said, and he must have meant the prince was to marry the sun woman. I am quite sure the king is much too proud to wish his son to marry anyone but a princess."

"I see what you are driving at now," said his mother.

"But," said his father, "our king would move the mountain to the plain before he would allow his princess to become the wife of a cob, even if the goblin were ten times a prince."

"Yes, but they think so much of themselves," said his mother. "Small creatures always do. The bantam is the proudest cock in my little yard."

"I fancy," said Curdie, "if they once got her, they would tell our king that they would kill her unless he consented to the marriage."

"They might say so," said his father, "but they wouldn't really kill her. They would keep her alive for the sake of the power it would give them over our king."

"And they are bad enough to torment her just for their own amusement. I know that," said Curdie's mother.

"Anyhow, I will keep a watch on them, and see what they are up to," said Curdie. "But they shan't have her—at least if I can help it. So Mother dear, if you will get me a bit of paper and a pencil and a lump of pease pudding, I will set out at once. I saw a place where I can climb over the wall of the garden quite easily."

"You must be careful to keep out of the way of the men-at-arms on the watch," said his mother.

"That I will. I don't want them to know anything about it, for that would spoil it all. The cobs are such obstinate creatures, they would only try some other plan. I shall take care, Mother."

His mother got him what he had asked for, and Curdie set out. Close beside the door by which the princess had left the garden for the mountain stood a great rock, and there Curdie climbed over the wall. He tied his string to a stone just inside the channel of the stream and took his pickaxe with him.

He had not gone far before he encountered a horrid creature coming towards him. The spot was too narrow for two of any size or shape to pass, nor did Curdie wish to let this creature by. Not being able to use his pickaxe, however, he had a severe struggle with him, and it was only after receiving many bites that he succeeded in killing the creature with his pocketknife. He dragged him outside and made haste to get in again before another creature should stop up the way.

By the time that Curdie had returned to his breakfast following the night's adventures, he was satisfied that the goblins were indeed mining in the direction of the palace. The level was so low that he thought their intention must be to burrow under the walls of the king's house, rise up inside, and lay hands upon the princess.

They meant to carry her off for a wife to their horrid Harelip.

## 24

# IRENE BEHAVES
# LIKE A PRINCESS

When the princess awoke, she found her nurse bending over her, the housekeeper looking over the nurse's shoulder, and the laundrymaid looking over the housekeeper's. The room was full of women-servants, and the gentlemen-at-arms, with a long column of servants behind them, were trying to peep in at the door of the nursery.

"Are those horrid creatures gone?" asked the princess, remembering what had terrified her in the first place.

"You naughty, naughty little princess," said Lootie.

Her face was very pale with red streaks in it, and she looked as if she were going to shake Irene. The princess said nothing—only waited to hear what would come next.

"How could you hide under the bed clothes like that and make us all fear you were lost? And keep it up all day too. You are the most obstinate child! It's anything but fun to us, I can tell you."

It was the only way the nurse could account for her disappearance.

"I didn't do that, Lootie," said Irene, very quietly.

"Don't tell stories," said Nurse quite harshly.

"Then I shall tell you nothing at all," said Irene.

"That's just as bad," said the nurse.

"Just as bad to say nothing at all as to tell stories?" exclaimed the princess. "I will ask my papa about that. He won't say so. And I don't think he will like for you to say so either."

"Tell me exactly what you mean," said Nurse, half angry with the princess, and half frightened at the possible consequences to herself.

"When I tell you the truth, Lootie," said the princess, who somehow did not feel at all angry, "and you say to me 'Don't tell stories,' then it seems I *must* tell stories before you will believe me."

"You are very rude, princess," said Nurse.

"It is you who are rude, Lootie. And I will not speak to you again until you are sorry. Why should I speak to you, when I know you will not believe me?" returned the princess. For she did know perfectly well that if she were to tell Lootie what she had been about, the more she went on to tell her, the less Nurse would believe her.

"You are the most provoking child," said Nurse. "You deserve to be well punished for your wicked behavior."

"Please, Mrs. Housekeeper," said the princess, "will you take me to *your* room and keep me until my king-papa comes? I will ask him to come as soon as he can."

Everyone stared at these words. And since the housekeeper was afraid of the nurse, she sought to patch matters up, saying, "I am sure, Princess, Nurse did not mean to be rude to you."

"I do not think my papa would wish me to have a nurse who spoke to me as Lootie does. If she thinks I tell lies, she had better either say so to my papa or go away. Sir Walter, will *you* take charge of me then?"

"With the greatest of pleasure, Princess," answered the captain of the gentlemen-at-arms, walking with his great stride into the room.

The crowd of servants made way for him, and he bowed low before the princess's bed. "I shall send my servant at once on the fastest horse in the stable to tell your king-papa that Your Royal Highness desires his presence. When you have chosen one of these under-servants to wait upon you, I shall order the room to be cleared."

"Thank you very much, Sir Walter," said the princess, and her eye glanced towards a rosy-cheeked girl who had lately come to the house as a scullery maid.

But when Lootie saw the eyes of her princess going in search of another servant instead of her, she fell upon her knees by the bedside and began to cry in distress.

"I think, Sir Walter," said the princess, "I will keep Lootie for now. But I put myself under your care, and you need not trouble my king-papa until I speak to you again. Will you all please go away? I am quite safe and well, and I did not hide myself for the sake either of amusing myself or of troubling my people."

## 25

# Curdie Comes to Grief

Everything was quiet above ground for some time. The king was away in a distant part of his dominions. The men-at-arms kept watch about the house. They had been astonished to find the hideous body of the goblin creature killed by Curdie lying at the foot of the rock in the garden, and they came to the conclusion that it had been slain in the mines and had crept outside to die.

Curdie himself kept watch inside the mountain as the goblins burrowed deeper into the earth. As long as they went deeper, Curdie judged there was no immediate danger.

To Irene the summer was as full of pleasure as ever. For a long time she thought of her grandmother during the day and dreamed about her at night, but she did not see her again. The goats and the flowers were her delight, and she made as much friends with the miners' children whom she met on the mountain as Lootie would permit. Lootie had strong notions about the dignity of a princess and did not understand that the truest princess is the one who humbly loves all her brothers and sisters best. At the same time Nurse was considerably altered for the better in her behavior to the princess. Lootie could see that Irene was no longer a mere child, but wiser than her age would account for. Lootie kept whispering to the servants that the princess was not right in her mind, sometimes that she was too good to live, and other nonsense of the same sort.

All this time Curdie was sorry that he had behaved so unkindly to the princess, yet he had no chance of confessing. This perhaps made him the more diligent in his endeavors to serve her. His mother and he often talked on the subject, and she comforted him with the certainty that he would some day have the opportunity he so much desired. He knew that it was a contemptible thing for a prince or princess to refuse to confess a fault or an error, so there may have been some ground for supposing that Curdie was not only a miner, but something of a prince as well.

At length as Curdie watched, he began to see changes in the proceedings of the goblin excavators. They were going no deeper, but instead had begun digging on a level. Curdie watched them more closely than ever. One night, coming to a slope of very hard rock, they began to ascend along the inclined plane of its surface. They reached its top and went again on a level for a night or two, and then began to ascend once more at a pretty steep angle.

Curdie judged it time to observe from another quarter, and the next night he did not go to the mine at all. He left his pickaxe and paper at home, and took only his usual lumps of bread and pease pudding down the mountain to the king's house. He climbed over the wall and remained in the garden the whole night, creeping on hands and knees from one spot to the other. He spread himself out at full length with his ear to the ground, listening. But he heard nothing except the tread of the men-at-arms as they marched about. He had little difficulty avoiding their observation, as the night was cloudy and there was no moon. For several nights he continued to haunt the garden and listen, but with no success.

Finally at length one evening, whether it was because he had gotten careless or that the growing moon had become strong enough to expose him, his watching came to a sudden end. He was creeping from behind the rock where the stream ran out, when just as he came into the moonlight on the lawn, a *whizz* in his ear and a blow upon his leg startled him. He instantly squatted in the hope of eluding further notice. But he heard the sound of running feet, and he jumped up to take flight and escape. He fell, however, when the bolt of a crossbow wounded his leg. Blood began to stream from the wound, and the pain was keen. He was instantly laid hold of by two or three of the men-at-arms. It was useless to struggle, and so he submitted in silence.

"It's a boy!" cried several of them together in amazement. "I thought it was one of those goblins. What are you doing here?"

"Getting a bit of rough usage apparently," said Curdie, as the men shook him.

"Impertinence will do you no good. You have no business here in the king's grounds, and if you don't give a true account of yourself, you shall fare as a thief."

"Why, what else could he be?" said one.

"He might have been searching for a lost goat, you know," suggested another.

"I see no good in trying to excuse him. He has no business here."

"Let me go away then, if you please," said Curdie.

"But we don't please—not until you give a good account of yourself."

"I don't feel quite sure whether I can trust you," said Curdie.

"We are the king's own men-at-arms," said the captain courteously, for he was taken with Curdie's appearance and courage.

"Then I will tell you all about it—if you will promise to listen to me and not do anything rash."

"I call that brash," said one of the party laughing. "He will tell us what mischief he was about, if we promise to do as pleases him."

"I was about no mischief," said Curdie.

But before he could say more, he fainted and fell senseless on the grass. It was then that they first discovered that the bolt they had shot thinking he was a goblin had wounded him.

They carried him into the house and laid him down in the hall. The report spread that they had caught a robber, and the servants crowded in to see the villain.

Among the rest came the nurse, and the moment she saw him she exclaimed with indignation, "I declare it's the same young rascal of a miner that was rude to me and the princess on the mountain. He actually wanted to kiss the princess. I took good care of that—the wretch! So he was prowling about, was he? Just like him."

When the captain heard this, he resolved to keep Curdie a prisoner until they could search into the affair and learn the truth. After they had brought him around a little and attended to his wound, which was rather a bad one, they laid him, still exhausted from the loss of blood, upon a mattress in a disused room and locked the door. He passed a troubled night, and in the morning they found him talking wildly. When he finally came to himself, he felt very weak, and his leg was exceedingly painful. Wondering where he was, and seeing one of the men-at-arms in the room, Curdie began to question him and soon recalled the events of the preceding night.

Since Curdie was himself unable to watch the goblins anymore, he told the soldier all he knew about them. He begged the man to tell his companions, and to stir them up to watch with tenfold vigilance. But whether Curdie did not talk coherently, or whether the whole thing appeared incredible, the man concluded that Curdie was raving still, and tried to coax him into holding his tongue. This, of course, annoyed Curdie dreadfully, who now felt in his turn what it was like not to be believed. The consequence was that his fever returned, and by the time the captain was called to hear his persistent entreaties, there could be no doubt that he was raving. They did for him what they could, and promised him everything he wanted—but with no intention of fulfillment.

At last he went to sleep again, and when at length his sleep grew profound and peaceful, they left him. They locked the door again, and withdrew, intending to revisit him early in the morning.

## 26

# THE GOBLIN MINERS

That same night several of the servants were having a chat together before going to bed when one of the housemaids said, "What can that noise be?"

"I've heard it the last two nights too," said the cook. "If there were any about the place, I would have taken it for rats."

"I've heard that rats move about in great companies sometimes," said the scullery maid, "Maybe an army of rats is invading us. I've heard the noises yesterday and today too."

"It'll be grand fun for my Tom and Bob then," said the cook. "For once in their lives they'll be friends and fight on the same side. I'll wager that together they will put to flight any number of rats."

"It seems to me," said Nurse, "that the noises are much too loud for rats. I have heard them all day, and my princess has asked me several times what they could be. Sometimes they sound like distant thunder, and sometimes like the noises you hear in the mountain from those horrid miners underneath."

"I shouldn't wonder," said the cook, "if it was the miners after all. They are always boring and blasting and breaking, you know."

Then there came a great rolling rumble beneath them, and the house quivered. They all rushed to the hall where they found the gentlemen-at-arms in consternation. They had sent to waken their captain. The captain said that from their description it must have been an earthquake—an occurrence which was very rare in that country, but one that had taken place earlier in the century. The captain returned to bed, and strange to say, he fell fast asleep without once thinking of Curdie. He must not have believed Curdie, for if he had, he would at once have thought of what he had been told and would have taken precautions.

The servants and men-at-arms heard nothing more, and so concluded that Sir Walter was right and that the danger was over for perhaps another hundred years.

The fact, as discovered afterwards, was that the goblins had arrived at a huge block which lay under the cellars of the house within the line of the foundations. It was so round that when they succeeded, after hard work, in dislodging it without blasting, it rolled thundering down the slope with a bounding, jarring roll, which shook the foundations of the house.

The goblins were themselves dismayed at the noise, for they knew by careful spying and measuring, that they must now be very near, if not right under the king's house, and they feared giving an alarm. They, therefore, remained quiet for quite a while. When they began to work again, they thought themselves very fortunate in coming upon a vein of sand which filled a winding fissure in the rock on which the house was built. By scooping the sand away, they came out in the king's wine cellar. As soon as they discovered where they were, they scurried back again like rats into their holes. Running at full speed to the goblin palace, they announced their success to the king and queen with shouts of triumph.

In only a moment the royal goblin family and all the rest of the goblins were on their way in haste to the king's house. Each was eager to have a share in the glory of carrying off that same night the Princess Irene.

The queen herself went stumping along in one shoe of stone and one of skin.

They soon arrived in the king's wine cellar. They did not know the use of the huge vessels, and so they proceeded at once as quietly as they could to force open the door that led upwards.

# 27

# THE GOBLINS
# IN THE KING'S HOUSE

When Curdie fell asleep, he began to dream that he was ascending the mountainside from the mouth of the mine, whistling and singing *Ring, dod, bang!* when he came upon a woman and child who had lost their way. From that point on he dreamt everything that had happened to him since he had first met the princess and Lootie on the path. He dreamed that he watched the goblins, that he was taken by them and then rescued by the princess. He dreamed everything, indeed, until he was wounded, captured, and imprisoned by the men-at-arms. And now he thought he was lying wide awake where they had laid him, when suddenly he heard a great thundering sound.

"The cobs are coming!" he said. "The men didn't believe a word I told them! The cobs'll be carrying the princess off from under their very noses! But they shan't!"

He jumped up—he thought—and began to dress. But to his dismay he found that he was still lying in bed.

"Now then, I will!" he said. "Here goes! I am up now!"

But yet again he found himself snug in bed. Twenty times he tried, and twenty times he failed. For in fact he was not awake, only dreaming that he was. At length in an agony of despair, fancying that he heard the goblins all over the house, he gave a great cry. Then there came—he thought—a hand on the lock of his door which opened. He looked up and saw a lady with white hair enter the room. She was carrying a silver box in her hand. She came to his bed—he thought—stroked his head and face with cool, soft hands, took the dressing off of his leg and rubbed it with something that smelled like roses. Then she waved her hands over him three times. At the last wave of her hands everything vanished. He felt himself sinking into the profoundest slumber and remembered nothing more until he awoke in earnest.

The setting moon was throwing a feeble light through the casement, and the house was full of uproar. There was the soft heavy stamping of many feet, a clashing and clanging of weapons, the voices of men and the cries of women, mixed with a hideous bellowing, which sounded victorious. The cobs were in the house!

Curdie sprang from his bed and hurried on some of his clothes, not forgetting his shoes, which were armed with nails. He spied an old short sword hanging on the wall, caught it up in his hand, and rushed down the stairs. He was guided by the sounds of strife, which grew louder and louder.

When he reached the ground floor, he found the whole place swarming.

All the goblins of the mountain seemed gathered there. He rushed amongst them, shouting.

"One, two,
Hit and hew!
Three, four,
Blast and bore!"

And with every rhyme he came down a great stamp upon a foot, cutting at the same time their faces, executing a sword dance of the wildest description. The goblins scattered away in every direction—into closets, up stairs, into chimneys, up on rafters, and down to the cellars. Curdie went on stamping and slashing and singing, but saw nothing of the people of the house until he came to the great hall.

The moment he entered the hall, a great goblin shout arose. The last man-at-arms and the captain himself were both on the floor, buried beneath a wallowing crowd of goblins. The knight was busy defending himself as well as he could, stabbing the thick bodies of the goblins. He had found the goblin heads all but invulnerable, and the queen had attacked his legs and feet with her horrible granite shoe. The captain had gotten his own back to the wall and stood out longer.

The goblins would have torn them all to pieces, but the king had given orders to carry them away alive. So in twelve groups a knot of goblins stood over each man-at-arms, while as many as could find room were sitting upon their prostrate bodies.

Curdie burst in dancing and slashing, stamping and singing like a small spinning whirlwind.

"Where 'tis all a hole, sir,
Never can be holes:
Why should their shoes have soles, sir,
When they've got no souls?

"But she upon her foot, sir,
Has a granite shoe:
The strongest leather boot, sir,
Six would soon be through."

The queen gave a howl of rage and dismay, and before she recovered her presence of mind, Curdie had eleven of the knights back up on their legs again.

"Stamp on their feet!" he cried as each man rose. And in a few minutes the hall was nearly empty with the goblins running from it as fast as they could. They were howling and shrieking and limping, as they ran to protect their wounded feet from the frightful *stamp-stamp* of the armed men.

Now Curdie approached the group which stood with the queen and her remaining shoe guarding the captain lying prostrate on the floor. The goblin king sat on the captain's head, and the queen stood in front like an infuriated cat with her perpendicular eyes gleaming green and her hair standing half up from her horrid head. Her heart was quaking, however, and she kept her unclad foot moving about with nervous apprehension. When Curdie was within a few paces, she rushed at him, made one tremendous stamp at his opposing foot, and caught him around the waist to dash him on the marble floor. Happily he withdrew his foot just in time, and came down instead with all the weight of his iron-shod shoe upon her unclad foot. With a hideous howl she dropped him, squatted on the floor, and took her foot in both her hands.

Meanwhile the rest rushed on the goblin king and his bodyguards, sent them flying, and lifted the prostrate captain, who was all but pressed to death. It was some moments before he recovered breath and consciousness.

"Where's the princess?" cried Curdie, again and again.

No one knew, so off they all rushed in search of her.

They went through every room in the house, but found her nowhere. Neither were any of the servants to be seen. But Curdie himself stayed in the lower part of the house, which was now quiet enough. He began to hear the sound of a distant hubbub, and he set out to find where it came from. The noise grew as his sharp ears guided him to a stair and then on to the wine cellar. It was full of goblins compelling the butler to supply them with wine as fast as he could draw it.

While the queen and her party had encountered the men-at-arms, Harelip had gone off with another company to search the house. They captured every servant they met, and when they could find no more, they hurried away to carry them safe to the caverns below. But when the butler, who was among the captives, found that their path lay through the wine cellar, he thought of tempting them to taste the wine. And, just as he had hoped, they no sooner tasted it than they wanted more. When Curdie entered, the goblins had abandoned all reason on the wine. They sat with outstretched hands, in which were vessels of every description from saucepan to silver cup, pressing the butler who sat at the tap of a huge cask for more and yet more.

Curdie cast one glance around the place before commencing his attack. He saw in the farthest corner a terrified group of the servants. They were unnoticed, but they cowered without courage to attempt even to escape. Among them was the terror-stricken face of Lootie, but nowhere could he see the princess. Curdie was seized with the horrible conviction that Harelip had already carried her off. He rushed in among the goblins, too angry to sing any more, but stamping and cutting with greater fury than ever before.

"Stamp on their feet; stamp on their feet!" he shouted, and in a moment the goblins were disappearing through the hole in the floor like rats and mice. They could not all vanish quickly, however, and many goblin feet went limping back into the underground passages of the mountain.

Presently the goblins in the cellar were reinforced from above by the king and his party, with the redoubtable queen and her shoe at their head. Finding Curdie again busy among her unfortunate subjects, the queen rushed at him once more, and this time gave him a bad bruise on the foot. Then a regular stamping fight commenced between them, Curdie, with the point of his hunting knife keeping her from clasping her mighty arms about him, while he watched for an opportunity to once more stamp on her unclad foot. But the queen was more wary this time as well.

The other goblins, finding their adversary Curdie thus matched for the moment, paused in their headlong hurry out of the cellar, and turned to the shivering group of women in the corner. Harelip rushed at them, caught up Lootie, and sped with her to the hole. She gave a great shriek—loud enough for Curdie to hear. He saw the plight she was in, and gathering all his strength gave the queen a sudden cut across the face with his weapon, came down with all his weight on the proper foot, and sprung to Lootie's rescue.

Prince Harelip had two defenseless feet, and on both of them Curdie stamped just as they reached the hole. Harelip dropped his burden and rolled shrieking into the earth. Curdie made one stab at him as he disappeared, caught hold of Lootie, and dragged her back to the corner. There he stood guard over her, preparing once more to encounter the queen.

Her green eyes flashed, and she came forward followed by the king and her bodyguard of the thickest goblins. But at the same moment, in rushed the captain and his men-at-arms. They ran at the goblins stamping furiously. Away they scurried, the queen foremost. Of course, the right thing would have been to take the goblin king and queen prisoners, and hold them hostages in exchange for the princess. But so anxious were they to find her that no one thought of detaining them until it was too late.

All set about searching the house once more, but none could find the least bit of information concerning the princess. Lootie was almost silly with terror, and would not leave Curdie's side for a single moment. He allowed the others to search the rest of the house where, except for a dismayed goblin lurking here and there, they found no one. He requested Lootie to take him to the princess's room. She was as submissive and obedient as if he had been the king.

He found the bedclothes tossed about, and most of them on the floor. The princess's garments too were scattered all over the room, which was in the greatest confusion. It was only too evident that the goblins had been there, and Curdie had no longer any doubt that she had been carried off at the very first of the invasion.

In despair he saw how wrong they had been in not securing the goblin king and queen and prince. But he determined to find and rescue the princess, just as she had found and rescued him, or meet the worst fate to which the goblins could doom him.

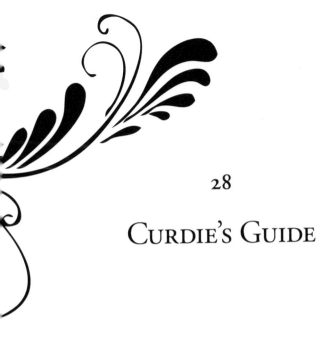

## 28

# CURDIE'S GUIDE

J ust as Curdie was comforted by this resolve, and was turning toward the cellar to follow the goblins into their hole, something touched his hand. It was the slightest touch, and when he looked he could see nothing. Feeling about in the gray of the dawn, his fingers came upon a tight thread. He looked again, and carefully, but still could see nothing. It flashed upon him that this must be the princess's thread.

Without saying a word, for he knew no one would believe him any more than he had believed her, he slipped away from Lootie and followed the thread with his finger. He was soon out of the house and on the mountainside. If the thread were indeed the grandmother's messenger, he supposed it would lead him into the mountain to the princess, where she was certain to meet the goblins rushing back enraged from their defeat.

He hurried on in the hope of overtaking the princess before the goblins could arrive. When he came to the place where the path turned off for the mine, however, he found that the thread did not turn, but went straight up the mountain. Could the thread be leading him home to his mother's cottage? Could the princess be there? He bounded up the mountain like one of its own goats, and before the sun was up, the thread had brought him indeed to his mother's door. And there it vanished from his fingers. He could not find it, search as he might.

The door was unlatched, and he entered. There sat his mother by the fire, and in her arms lay the princess, fast asleep.

"Hush, Curdie," said his mother. "Do not wake her. I'm so glad you're come. I thought the cobs must have got you again."

With a heart full of delight, Curdie sat down on a stool at a corner of the hearth, opposite his mother's chair. He gazed at the princess, who slept as peacefully as if she was in her own bed. All at once she opened her eyes and fixed them on him.

"Oh, Curdie, you're come," she said quietly. "I thought you would."

Curdie rose and stood before her with downcast eyes.

"Irene," he said, "I am very sorry I did not believe you before."

"You couldn't, you know, Curdie," answered the princess. "But you do believe me now, don't you?"

"I can't help it now, and I ought to have helped it before."

"Why can't you help it now?"

"Because just as I was going into the mountain to look for you, I got hold of your thread, and it brought me here."

"Then you've come from my house?"

"Yes, I have."

"I didn't know you were there."

"I've been there two or three days, I believe."

"I never knew it. Then perhaps you can tell me why my grandmother has brought me here? I can't think. Something woke me—I didn't know what, but I was frightened. I felt for the thread, and there it was! I was more frightened still when it brought me out on the mountain, for I thought it was going to take me inside it again, and I like the outside of it best. I supposed you were in trouble again, and that I had to get you out. But it brought me here instead. Oh, Curdie, your mother has been so kind to me—just like my own grandmother!"

Here Curdie's mother gave the princess a hug, and the princess turned and gave her a sweet smile.

"Then you didn't see the cobs?" asked Curdie.

"No. I haven't been into the mountain. I told you, Curdie."

"But the cobs have been into your house—all over it—and into your bedroom, making such a row!"

"That was very rude of them. What did they want there?"

"They wanted you. They wanted to carry you off into the mountain with them to become a wife to their prince Harelip."

"Oh, how dreadful," said the princess, shuddering.

"But you needn't be afraid, you know. Your grandmother takes care of you."

"Ah! you do believe in my grandmother, then? I'm so glad! She made me think you would some day."

All at once Curdie remembered his dream and was silent, thinking.

"But how did you come to be in my house, and me not know it?" asked the princess.

Then Curdie explained everything—how he had watched for her sake, how he had been wounded and shut up by the soldiers, how he heard the noises and could not rise, and how the beautiful old lady had come to him, and all that followed.

"Poor Curdie, to lie there hurt and ill, and me never to know it!" exclaimed the princess, stroking his rough hand. "I would have come and helped you, if they had told me."

"I didn't see that you were lame," said his mother.

"Am I, Mother? I haven't thought of it since I went among the cobs."

"Let me see your wound," said his mother.

He pulled down his stocking, and except a great scar, his leg was perfectly sound!

Curdie and his mother gazed in each other's eyes, full of wonder, but Irene called out, "I thought so, Curdie. I was sure it wasn't a dream. I was sure my grandmother has been to see you. Don't you smell the roses? It was my grandmother healed your leg and sent you to help me."

"No, Princess Irene," said Curdie, "I am not good enough to be allowed to help you. I didn't believe you. Your grandmother took care of you without me."

"She sent you to help my people anyhow. I wish my king-papa would come. I do want so to tell him how good you have been!"

"But," said Curdie's mother, "we are forgetting how frightened your people must be. You must take the princess home, Curdie—or at least go and tell them where she is."

"I will, Mother. Only they ought to have listened to me, and then they wouldn't have been taken by surprise as they were."

"That is true, Curdie, but it is not for you to blame them much. You remember?"

"Yes, Mother, I do."

"Do have some breakfast, and then leave at once. You must be dreadfully hungry, my boy." said his mother, rising and setting the princess on her chair.

But before a breakfast could be made ready, Curdie jumped up suddenly startling both his companions.

"Mother!" he cried, "I was forgetting. You must take the princess home yourself. I must go and wake my father."

Without a word of explanation, he rushed to his father's bed. Having thoroughly roused him with what he told him, he darted out of the cottage.

## 29

# MASONWORK

Curdie had suddenly remembered that the goblins would carry out their second plan upon the failure of the first. And no doubt they were already busy. The mine was in great danger of being flooded and rendered useless—not to speak of the lost lives of the miners.

When he reached the mouth of the mine, after rousing all the miners within reach, he found his father and a good many more just entering. They all hurried to the gang by which he had found a way into the goblin country. There, through the foresight of Peter, were a great many blocks of stone and cement, ready for building up the weak place—a place known well enough to the goblins. There was room enough for no more than two to be building at once. All the rest went to work preparing the cement and passing the stones into the gang. By day's end the miners had finished constructing a huge buttress supported everywhere by the new rock, and so before the hour when they usually stopped their work, they were satisfied that the mine was secure.

They had heard goblin hammers and pickaxes busy all the time, and they fancied that they heard sounds of water they had never heard before. But the water was accounted for when they left the mine, for they stepped out into a tremendous rainstorm raging all over the mountain. The thunder was bellowing, and the lightning was lancing out of a huge black cloud which lay above the mountain and hung thick mist down over its edges. From the state of the brooks, now swollen into raging torrents, it was evident that the storm had been raging all day.

The wind was blowing with enough force to blow him off the mountain, but Curdie was anxious about his mother and the princess, and he darted up into the thick of the tempest. He did not judge them safe, for in such a storm their poor little house was in danger. Indeed he soon found that it would have been swept away had it not been for the huge rock which protected it both from the blasts and the waters. Two torrents of water rushing down the mountainside were parted by this rock, then rushed to unite again in front of the cottage—two roaring and dangerous streams, which his mother and the princess could not possibly have crossed. It was with great difficulty that Curdie forced his way through one of them and up to the door.

The moment his hand fell on the latch, through all the uproar of winds and waters came the joyous cry of the princess, "There's Curdie!"

She was sitting wrapped in blankets on the bed, his mother trying for the hundredth time to light the fire which had been drowned by the rain coming in down the chimney. The clay floor was one mass of mud, and the whole place looked wretched. But the faces of the mother and the princess shone as if their troubles only made them the merrier. Curdie burst out laughing at the sight of them.

"I never had such fun," said the princess, her eyes twinkling and her pretty teeth shining. "How nice it must be to live in a cottage on the mountain."

"It all depends on what kind your house is inside," said the mother.

"I know what you mean," said Irene. "That's the kind of thing my grandmother says."

By the time Peter returned, the storm was nearly over, but the streams were so fierce and so swollen that it was not only out of the question for the princess to go down the mountain, but most dangerous for even Peter or Curdie to attempt in the gathering darkness.

"They will be dreadfully frightened about you," said Peter to the princess, "but we cannot help it. We must wait until morning."

With Curdie's help, the fire was lighted at last, and his mother set about making their supper. After supper they all told the princess stories until she grew sleepy. Then Curdie's mother laid her in Curdie's bed in a tiny little garret room. As soon as she was in bed, through a little window low down in the roof she caught sight of her great-great-grandmother's lamp shining far away, and she gazed at the beautiful silvery globe until she fell asleep.

# 30

# THE KING AND THE KISS

The next morning the sun rose so bright that Irene said the rain had washed his face and let the light out clean. The torrents were still roaring down the side of the mountain, but they were much smaller and not so dangerous now in the daylight. After an early breakfast, Peter went to his work in the mine, and Curdie and his mother set out to take the princess home. They had difficulty in getting her dry across the streams, and Curdie again and again had to carry her, but at last they got safely to the broader part of the road. They walked gently down towards the king's house. And what should they see as they turned the last corner but the last of the king's troop riding through the gate!

"Oh, Curdie!" cried Irene, clapping her hands right joyfully, "my king-papa is come."

The moment Curdie heard that, he picked her up in his arms, and set off at full speed, calling out, "Come on, Mother dear! The king's heart may break until he knows that she is safe."

Irene clung to Curdie's neck, and he ran with her like a deer. When he entered the gate into the courtyard, there sat the king on his horse with all the people of the house about him, weeping and hanging their heads. The king himself was not weeping, but his face was as white as a dead man's, and he looked as if the life had gone out of him. The men-at-arms he had brought with him sat with horror-stricken faces. Their eyes were flashing with rage, waiting only for the word of the king to do something—they did not know what; nobody knew what.

On the day before the men-at-arms belonging to the house at last became satisfied that the princess had been carried away. By the time they rushed after the goblins into the hole, however, they found that the cobs had already skillfully blockaded the narrowest part not many feet below the cellar, and without miners and their tools they could do nothing. Not one of them knew where the mouth of the mine lay, and some of those who had set out to find it had been overtaken by the storm and had not even yet returned. Sir Walter was especially filled with shame, and almost hoped the king would order his punishment, for to think of that sweet little face down among the goblins was unbearable.

And so when Curdie ran in at the gate with the princess in his arms, they were all so absorbed in their own misery and awed by the king's presence and grief, that no one observed his arrival. He went straight up to the king, where he sat on his horse.

"Papa! Papa!" the princess cried, stretching out her arms to him, "here I am!"

The king started. The color rushed to his face, and he voiced a quiet cry. Curdie held the princess up, and the king bent over, took her from his arms, and clasped her to himself. Big tears began to drop down his cheeks into his beard.

Such a shout arose from all the bystanders that the startled horses pranced and capered, the armor rang and clattered, and the rocks of the mountain echoed back the noises.

The princess greeted them all as she nestled in her father's arms, and the king did not set her down until she had told them all the whole story. But she had more to tell about Curdie than about herself, and what she did tell about herself none of them could understand—none except for the king and Curdie, who stood by the king's knee stroking the neck of the great white horse. While she told what Curdie had done, Sir Walter and others added to what she told, and even Lootie joined in the praises of his courage.

Curdie held his peace, looking quietly up into the king's face. His mother stood on the outskirts of the crowd listening with delight, for her son's deeds were pleasant in her ears. Then the princess caught sight of her.

"And there is his mother, King-Papa!" she said. "See—there. She is such a nice mother and has been so kind to me!"

They all parted asunder as the king made a sign for her to come forward. She obeyed, and he gave her his hand, but could not speak.

"And now, King-Papa," the princess went on, "I must tell you another thing. One night long ago Curdie drove the goblins away and brought Lootie and me safe from the mountain. I promised him a kiss when we got home, but Lootie wouldn't let me give it to him. I don't want you to scold Lootie, but I want you to tell her that a princess must do as she promises."

"Indeed she must, my child—except it be wrong," said the king. "There now, give Curdie a kiss."

And as he spoke he held her towards him.

The princess reached down, threw her arms around Curdie's neck, and kissed him, saying, "There, Curdie! There's the kiss I promised!"

Then they all went into the house, and the cook rushed to the kitchen and the servants to their work. Lootie dressed Irene in her most beautiful clothes, and the king put off his armor and put on purple and gold. A messenger was sent for Peter and all the miners, and there was a great and a grand feast, which continued long after the princess was put to bed.

31

# THE SUBTERRANEAN WATERS

The king's harper, who always formed a part of the king's escort, was composing a ballad as he played on his instrument—about the princess and the goblins, and the prowess of Curdie. All at once he ceased, and his eyes were fixed on one of the doors of the hall.

Thereupon the eyes of the king and his guests turned also. Through the open doorway came Princess Irene. She went straight up to her father with her right hand stretched out a little sideways and her forefinger, as her father and Curdie understood, feeling its way along the invisible thread. The king took her on his knee, and she said in his ear, "King-Papa, do you hear that noise?"

"I hear nothing," said the king.

"Listen," she said, holding up her forefinger.

The king listened, and a great stillness fell upon the company. Each man, seeing that the king listened, listened also.

The harper sat with his harp between his arms, and his finger silent upon the strings.

"I do hear a noise," said the king at length, "a noise as of distant thunder. It is coming nearer and nearer. What can it be?"

They all heard it now, and each seemed ready to start to his feet as he listened. Yet all sat perfectly still. The noise came rapidly nearer.

"What can it be?" said the king again.

"I think it must be another storm coming over the mountain," said Sir Walter.

Then Curdie, who at the first word of the king had slipped from his seat and laid his ear to the ground, rose up quickly, and approached the king.

"Please, Your Majesty, I think I know what it is. I have no time to explain, for that might make it too late for some of us. Will Your Majesty give orders that everybody leave the house as quickly as possible and get up the mountain?"

The king, who was the wisest man in the kingdom, knew well that there was a time when things must be done and questions left till afterwards. He had faith in Curdie, and he rose instantly with Irene in his arms. "Every man and woman follow me," he said, and strode out into the darkness.

Before he had reached the gate, the noise had grown to a great thundering roar, and the ground trembled beneath their feet. And before the last of them had crossed the courtyard, out from the great hall door came a huge rush of turbid water. But they all got safely out of the gate and up the mountain, while the torrent went roaring down the road into the valley beneath.

Curdie had left the king and Irene to look after his mother. Now Curdie and his father, one on each side of her, caught her up when the stream overtook them and carried her safe and dry.

When the king had got out of the way of the water, a little up the mountain, he stood with the princess in his arms and looked back with amazement on the gushing torrent, which glimmered fierce and foamy through the night. There Curdie rejoined them.

"Now, Curdie," said the king, "what does this mean? Is this what you expected?"

"It is, Your Majesty," said Curdie. And he proceeded to tell him about the second scheme of the goblins, who had resolved, if they failed in carrying off the king's daughter, to flood the mine and drown the miners. Then he explained what the miners had done to prevent it.

The goblins had followed their design and let loose all the underground reservoirs and streams expecting the water to run down into the mine. They had not known of the solid wall close behind their chosen passage. But the readiest outlet the water could find had turned out to be the tunnel they had made into the king's house. And that catastrophic possibility had not occurred to the young miner until he had laid his ear to the floor of the hall and knew that all must leave immediately. The house appeared in danger of falling, and every moment the torrent was increasing.

"We must continue up the mountain at once," said the king. "But how to get at the horses?"

"Shall I see if we can manage that?" said Curdie.

"Do," said the king.

Curdie gathered the men-at-arms and took them back over the garden wall to the stables. They found their horses in terror with the water rising fast around them. It was quite time they were got out, but there was no way except to ride them directly through the water which was now pouring out of the lower windows as well as through the door. One horse was quite enough for any man to manage through such a torrent, and Curdie got on the king's white charger. Leading the way, he brought them all in safety to the higher ground.

"Look, Curdie!" cried Irene, the moment that he dismounted and led the horse up to the king.

Curdie did look and saw high in the air, over the top of the king's house, a great globe of light shining like the purest silver.

"Oh, no," he said in some consternation, "that is your grandmother's lamp! We must get her out. I will go and find her. The house may fall, you know."

"My grandmother is in no danger," said Irene, smiling.

"Here, Curdie, take the princess while I get on my horse," said the king.

Curdie took the princess again, and both turned their eyes to the globe of light. The same moment a white bird shot from it, descended with outstretched wings and made one circle around the king, Curdie, and the princess. It glided up again, and then the light and the pigeon vanished together.

"See, Curdie?" said the princess, as he lifted her to her father's arms, "My grandmother knows all about it, and she isn't frightened."

"My child," said the king, "you will be cold if you haven't something more on. Run, Curdie, my boy, and fetch anything you can lay your hands on to keep the princess warm. We have a long ride before us."

Curdie was gone in a moment, and soon returned with a great rich fur, and the news that dead goblins were tossing about in the current through the house. They had been caught in their own snare. Instead of flooding the mine, they had flooded their own country, and they were now swept up and drowned. Irene shuddered, but the king held her close. Then he turned to Sir Walter, and said, "Bring Curdie's father and mother here."

When they stood before him, the king said, "I wish to take your son with me. He shall enter my bodyguard at once and await further promotion."

Peter and his wife, overcome, only murmured almost inaudible thanks.

But Curdie spoke aloud. "Please, Your Majesty," he said, "I cannot leave my father and mother."

"That's right, Curdie," said the princess. "I wouldn't if I was you."

The king looked at the princess and then at Curdie with a glow of satisfaction on his countenance.

"I too think you are right, Curdie," he said, "and I will not ask you again. But I shall find a way to do something for you sometime."

"Your Majesty has already allowed me to serve you," said Curdie.

"Curdie, you should go with the king," said his mother, "We can get on very well without you."

"But I can't get on very well without you," said Curdie. "The king is very kind, but I could not be half the use to him that I am to you. Please, Your Majesty, all I ask is this. A warm, red petticoat for my mother? I would have gotten her one long ago, but for the goblins."

"As soon as we get home," said the king, "Irene and I will search out the warmest one to be found and send it by one of the gentlemen."

"Yes, that we will, Curdie," said the princess. "And soon we'll come back and see you wear it, Curdie's mother. Shan't we, King-Papa?"

"Yes, my love. I hope so," said the king.

Then turning to the miners, the king said, "Will you do the best you can for my servants tonight? I hope they will be able to return to the house tomorrow."

The miners with one voice promised their hospitality. Then the king commanded his servants to mind whatever Curdie should say to them, and after shaking hands with him and his father and mother, the king and the princess and his company rode away down the side of the new stream, which had already devoured half the road, into the starry night.

## 32

# THE LAST CHAPTER

All the rest went up the mountain and separated in groups to the homes of the miners. Curdie and his father and mother took Lootie with them. And the whole way, a light shone upon their path. But when they looked around they could see nothing of the silvery globe. All understood its origin save Lootie.

For days and days the water continued to rush from the doors and windows of the king's house, and a few goblin bodies were swept out into the road.

Curdie saw that something must be done. He spoke to his father and the rest of the miners, and at once they proceeded to make another outlet for the waters. By setting all hands to the work, tunneling here and building there, they soon succeeded. They made another tunnel to drain the water away from under the king's house, where they were soon able to get into the wine cellar. There they found a multitude of dead goblins—among the rest the queen, with one unclad foot and one shoe of stone. The water had swept away the miners' barricade and had greatly widened the passage. They rebuilt it securely, and then went back to their labors in the mine.

A good many of the goblins with their creatures escaped from the inundation out upon the mountain. Most of them soon left that part of the country, and of those who remained many grew milder in character; and indeed their skulls became softer as well as their hearts, and their feet grew harder. By degrees they became friendly with the inhabitants of the mountain and even with the miners who were merciless to the remaining cob creatures, until at length they all but disappeared.

And so the tale is told. The rest of the history of the Princess and Curdie must be kept for another volume.